Unashamed

the **Shameless** *trilogy*

Shameless
Shameful
UnAshamed

Unashamed

M. MALONE
NANA MALONE

Chapter One

The best snipers knew that the secret to the perfect shot was all mental. Great marksmanship required mastery of your own senses. Even in the middle of a firefight, you learned to shut out everything but the sound of your own heartbeat. There was a moment when everything was quiet, all was still and you had complete and total focus.

As Noah Blake surveyed the remnants of his destroyed office, his mind blocked out everything but the task at hand. He couldn't think about the fact that Matthias had been beaten almost to a pulp. He had to temporarily forget about Oskar's dislocated shoulder and that Jonas had been gassed and could possibly lose his sight.

He definitely couldn't remember the image of Lucia sobbing on the bed after almost being kidnapped or the fact that if he'd been sixty seconds later, she'd have been lost to him. Noah tensed and pushed the mental image into a closet and locked the door.

Not going there.

"Jonas, keep rinsing your eyes. The doctor is on his way."

His friend gave him a thumbs up and splashed more water in his eyes as he stood over the sink in the kitchen. Oskar sat at the counter, resting his arm on the surface while holding an ice pack to his shoulder. He'd probably be back to normal before any of the others. Noah had already popped the arm back in socket but it would be sore as hell for a few days. The doctor was going to give him hell for doing it himself, but Oskar had been suffering and they'd all had something dislocated at some point. He wasn't going to leave his friend in agony when he could fix the problem. Too bad he couldn't do something to help the others. He hated feeling so helpless.

Noah knelt next to where Matthias was stretched out on the floor and placed another ice pack against his jaw. His face had already swollen beyond belief, the eyelids so puffy his face was unrecognizable. It was a miracle the kid was still conscious. Noah suspected it was pure force of will because Matthias would hate the idea of being unconscious and at the mercy of others.

"I wish you weren't so fucking stubborn, kid. You need to be in the hospital."

"No way. Not putting you at risk."

His words were muffled and slurred, but Noah could easily understand him. Mainly because he'd known what Matthias would say even before he spoke. With how paranoid the kid was about his information being in the system, he'd have to be literally kissing the Grim Reaper before he'd consent to being hospitalized. Looking at his swollen, distorted features, Noah honestly thought he wasn't too far from that scenario. He looked bad. *Really* bad.

"Fuck putting us at risk. This is your life, Matthias. We can find a way to keep the heat off of us. We'll say you were mugged or something. Shit."

"No hospital. Please."

It was the please that did him in. He could feel the waves of panic coming off the other man. Nothing short of knocking him out completely would get Matthias through the doors of a hospital, and Noah didn't have the heart to put him through any more traumas.

"Doctor is here."

He looked up with relief at the sound of Ryan's voice. The only stroke of luck so far had been that Dylan and Ryan hadn't been in the office when they'd been hit so they were available to help out. Well, maybe it wasn't luck. The asshole who'd taken out half his team had probably known damn well exactly how many people were in the building. He seemed to have planned it all out. The only thing he hadn't counted on was Lucia.

Noah glanced over to the couch where she'd been sitting for the past ten minutes. She'd been inconsolable at first, clinging to him with all her strength, but now she was disturbingly silent. He'd tried to talk to her but was met with a blank stare each time. He wasn't sure if she was going into shock but in the midst of all the other physical injuries, he'd had no choice but to just keep her in his eyesight while he tried to take care of everyone else.

Jonas had told him that she'd refused to run. It

enraged him that she'd put her life in danger, but he couldn't deny that he was also proud as hell that she was so courageous. Not that he wasn't going to paddle her ass later for that stunt.

"Where should I start?" Dr. Breckner's eyes flared slightly when he took in Matthias's appearance. He moved forward without waiting for an answer.

Noah stood back so the doctor could examine him. The doctor had been their on-call physician for years, but they'd never had to call him for anything this severe. It was usually stab wounds, cracked ribs, or the rare graze of a bullet. Matthias looked like he was sporting all of the above and then some.

A young woman, probably only a little older than Lucia, approached her. "Hi, my name is Robin. I'm a nurse with Dr. Breckner. Are you injured?"

Lucia shook her head. The nurse glanced over at Noah uncertainly. He really wanted to argue, but something about the set of Lucia's mouth made him rethink trying to force her just then. Noah motioned for Robin to assist Jonas.

"Jonas, there's a nurse here to take a look at your eyes."

His friend blinked rapidly but gave a thumbs up to

show that he'd heard. Apparently he still couldn't see anything. *Fuck.* The nurse approached, speaking in low tones. Satisfied that the medical professionals had things in hand, Noah approached the couch where Lucia sat staring at the wall.

"Lucia, you really should let the doctor examine you."

She didn't move or acknowledge his words in any way. Noah put his arm around her shoulders and she flinched. His heart sank. God, she looked so small and vulnerable sitting here all alone, but it looked like she didn't want his comfort. Not that he blamed her. If he hadn't been so damned insistent on going to see Ian tonight then he would have been here to protect her. It was the same thing over and over again.

He just kept letting her down.

Then his mind flashed to Lucia curled up on the bed sobbing her heart out and his blood chilled for a totally new reason. He had no idea what that bastard had done to her before he'd gotten there. Had he ... touched her? She was showing some of the signs of sexual assault, especially not wanting to be touched.

Dylan waved at him, trying to get his attention. Noah thrust his hands through his hair roughly, taking out his frustration on the strands. The pain centered him, bringing him back to the present. He had a team of people counting on him to get them through the storm and to safety. A team that included Lucia. Their safety was paramount so he had to get his head out of his ass.

"I'll be right back, princess." He murmured the words to her without expecting a response so he was shocked as hell when she nodded.

"Please tell me you have some good news," he growled as he approached Dylan.

The other man blew out a breath. "I found a place that's big enough. It's not exactly up to our usual standards but maybe that's a good thing in this case. It's underground."

Noah looked around at the marvel of glass and steel that had been his pride and joy and a symbol of everything he'd overcome. In the end, it had been a weakness because of all the glass and how open it was. When they rebuilt, he was going for bulletproof glass for sure. In the meantime, going underground was perfect. It wasn't going to look like much but it would be a rock solid hideout while his team recovered and he spent some time in the trenches to smoke out the bastard targeting them.

Lucia. Targeting Lucia. Because he couldn't forget

for one moment what this was really about.

"Then underground we go."

Lucia's eyes followed the movement of the light the doctor flashed in them. She blinked to clear the halos from her vision before allowing him to listen to her heart. The nurse had already taken her blood pressure. All the while Noah watched from the background like a silent sentinel, looking like he would slaughter anything that so much as startled her.

For once, his watchfulness didn't annoy her. It was actually comforting to have someone else taking charge because she was operating strictly on autopilot. Oxygen in. Oxygen out. Blink. Swallow. Smile. She could only hope her expressions and reactions were appropriate because inside she was spinning out. The whole world as she knew it had been scrambled and then put in a blender.

How could she care about anything when it was possible she'd lost hold on reality?

She'd heard him. She'd heard her brother's voice in

that room and nothing would ever be the same again.

Lucia glanced around frantically, afraid that the others could hear her thoughts or somehow read the truth on her face. She took a deep breath, but nothing could stop the slew of memories. A fun-filled day at Coney Island. Rafe smiling at her over funnel cake. Rafe on the ground covered with blood. Years of pain missing half of her heart.

Then a voice in the dark that she'd thought never to hear again.

Lucia had to restrain the urge to start screaming at the top of her lungs. She couldn't show that she was freaking out because Noah wouldn't understand. Her breath started to come faster despite trying to control it. It was all too much and she couldn't hold it in. The voices were too loud; the slide of fabric over her skin was too rough. Even the air smelled strange.

Everything was all wrong, and she feared if she made one wrong move she'd crack into a million pieces.

Being in a new place didn't help. The past three hours were a blur, but somehow Noah had gotten them all moved to a new location; some dark lair underground with bare walls and no furniture. Someone with a truck must have come as they were leaving because the couch in the middle of the room was the same one she'd been sitting on at the old place. How that was possible she wasn't sure, although apparently anything was possible with enough money.

"You don't have a concussion, Miss DeMarco and your vitals are strong. If you need something to help you sleep, I can give you a shot. Is there any chance that you could be pregnant?"

Her eyes shot over to Noah in surprise. His stance didn't change but there was no hiding the slight tension around his eyes. Even under these strange circumstances, Lucia blushed. After everything they'd done to and with each other, it was ridiculous that *this* could make her blush.

"No, I'm on the pill."

"Excellent. I can give you—"

Lucia held up her hand. "I don't need anything." Although she knew she wasn't going to sleep now or anytime soon, the last thing she wanted was something that would mess with her mind. She needed to keep her mind sharp. It was hard enough already to determine what was real.

The doctor smiled in that detached way all medical professionals must learn in school. "Okay. Just keep the lacerations on your feet clean and dry. The stitches in your right foot will start to dissolve within a week."

Lucia had already forgotten about the cuts on her feet. The memory of running across glass was muted by everything that had come afterward. What were a few slices on her feet compared to what the others had gone through? She climbed down carefully from the makeshift examining table Noah had set up in one of the spare rooms. Out in the hallway, she paused at the door of the room where Matthias rested while the same nurse who'd tried to help her, Robin or something like that, monitored the equipment hooked up to him.

"He should be in the hospital," she muttered, feeling guilty as hell.

She'd truly thought Matthias was dead after watching that brutal fight. That he'd managed to hold his own was a miracle. Although it had been a shock to see him in that full-on, aggressive mode. It had made his behavior at the fashion show seem like child's play in comparison. To think, she'd been shocked then just to see him handle a gun.

Noah followed her as she turned away and walked back toward the main room. "Are you sure you don't want the sedative, Lucia? You've been through a lot tonight. You were almost kidnapped."

"I'm aware, Noah. I was there, remember?" Lucia immediately regretted her sharp tone, especially when she saw his wince.

The silence between them was fraught with all the things she couldn't say aloud. So many questions. Why did you leave me alone? Who keeps trying to kill me?

Am I losing my mind?

He was trying so hard to be considerate with her and she was being so bitchy. But her mind was a mass of feelings and some of them weren't fair to Noah. Part of her was angry with him because he hadn't kept her safe even as she realized that was unfair. He wasn't infallible and if he'd been there, he'd likely be hurt just like the others.

"Sorry, I'm just wound up from everything."

"No, I'm sorry," Noah mumbled. "I just don't want you to suffer needlessly. You've already suffered enough. All I've ever wanted was to protect you. But I can't even do that."

He walked past her toward the kitchen. The new place was laid out completely differently than the old one. It was only one level with exposed brick walls and no windows. It was dark and cold and ugly. Fitting for how she felt. Lucia sat on the couch, happy to have this little bit of familiarity in the middle of everything. She watched as Noah waved two men through carrying a mattress. It was mind boggling to think of all the details he'd had to handle in order to get them set up in a new place so fast.

Thankful that he had it all under control, she burrowed deeper into the cushions of the couch, resolved to ignore it all. She didn't want to think about Matthias fighting for his life in one of the spare bedrooms or Jonas with his head wrapped in gauze, looking like a mummy.

Seeing the physical evidence of tonight was just one more thing to make her feel guilty. Her friends, her family, were in various stages of injury because of her. Whoever was targeting them was fixated on *her*. She'd started digging into the past and sifting through secrets that were apparently more dangerous than she could have imagined. Now they were paying the price.

An hour later, Lucia lifted her head and listened. It was noticeably quieter. Ryan came out of one of the rooms and nodded a silent greeting. She waved and then walked in the other direction. When Noah had been in full on alpha wolf mode earlier, she'd heard him barking out orders, specifically telling Ryan and Dylan that they needed to stay on site until further notice.

When she passed Matthias's room, the steady beep of the machines followed her down the hall. Behind the last door on the end, Noah sat on the bed with his head in his hands. He looked up when she entered the room.

"Your things are in the bathroom. I had them bring everything on the counter."

"Luckily I didn't have much at your place. What happens to the rest of your stuff?"

He shook his head slightly. "I have someone working through the night to box up everything. We'll have it all within twenty-four hours."

That was good. She hadn't wanted to think about him losing everything he owned just because he'd had the misfortune of helping her.

"Lucia, if something happened…" He stopped and wiped a hand over his face. "You can tell me anything. I'm not sure how long he had you in there before I found you—"

His voice cracked slightly and Lucia rushed forward and wrapped her arms around him.

"Noah, I'm fine. He didn't do anything. I mean, not what you're thinking. You got there in time." She repeated it several times because it seemed to soothe him.

Guilty that her silence had fostered his fears, she continued to stroke his hair gently. She suspected that Noah hadn't enjoyed a lot of softness in his life, and he seemed to drink up her affection like a thirsty plant. She would never want him to suffer any longer than necessary worrying that she'd been hurt or assaulted.

A huge yawn broke the silence and took Lucia by surprise. Despite everything that had happened, she didn't actually feel tired. The adrenaline in her system kept her on edge, making her cranky and fidgety. However her body seemed to be on a completely different schedule than her mind because she was suddenly so exhausted she wasn't sure she had the energy to even undress for bed.

Noah, as always, seemed to know what she needed before she did. "Raise your hands, princess. Let's get you out of these clothes and into bed."

She let him undress her, quiet and docile as a child. When he'd finally stripped her out of the shirt and jeans, she climbed between the sheets, letting out a deep sigh when her face met the pillow. It smelled like him, like Noah, and she realized they must have moved the mattress and pillow with all of the original bedding still on it. She wasn't sure why that struck her as so funny but suddenly she was laughing so hard she couldn't breathe.

The laughter went on and on until she was spent. When she glanced over at Noah, she braced herself for him to be annoyed or disgusted with her. Their friends were injured, their home was destroyed and she was laughing. Except when she saw his face it wasn't disgusted. He watched her with an expression that could only be pity. He brushed her cheek with his thumb and when Lucia saw the moisture there it shocked the hell out of her.

She was crying.

Chapter Two

A few days later, Noah sat carefully on the edge of

the bed and watched Lucia sleep. He was exhausted but finally everyone was settled for the night and he was the only one still awake. She shifted slightly, her lips parting as she let out a small sigh.

God, she is so beautiful just like this. Her dark hair spilled over the pillowcase like a riot of satin ribbons. He touched her cheek gently, unable to resist the urge to touch her when she wasn't awake. When he couldn't see the look of disappointment in her eyes. Problem was, she wouldn't talk to him.

The doctor had said she'd recover physically. The lacerations on her feet and hands would heal. The bruises would fade. But she wasn't talking. What's more, she wasn't yelling. He was used to Lucia giving him hell. But lately, it was an accomplishment to get any kind of reaction out of her. Most of the time, if she was awake, her eyes were blank and vacant.

Noah ran a hand through his hair in frustration. It was killing him to see her like this, so cut off from everything and everyone. She'd retreated into her own world and there wasn't anything he could do about it. Or at least nothing he'd tried so far had worked. It was like the lights were on but whoever was in there refused to answer the door for fear of solicitors.

What the hell had happened? She said she hadn't been assaulted, but *something* was happening with her. He closed his eyes and tried to focus, to remember exactly what he'd seen. His memories were a jumble of fear, horror and then pure rage. He didn't even like remembering. He'd walked into what looked like the set of a horror movie with bodies strewn all over the place and broken glass glittering on the floor like diamonds.

Then he'd heard Lucia screaming.

By the time he'd followed the sound to their room, all he'd seen was that walking corpse—because the guy was as good as dead as far as he was concerned—holding her way too tightly as Lucia struggled in his arms. He hadn't assaulted her, but there were a million ways to hurt someone. And he knew them all. Had that piece of shit hurt her before Noah had gotten there?

Had he tortured her by telling her what he was planning to do? Noah had no idea. So of course he couldn't fix it, because for once in their lives, Lucia wasn't giving him hell.

"Lucia, wake up princess." He repeated it softly over and over until she stirred.

She let out a soft sigh and then rolled over. Her eyes blinked open and she stilled when she saw him sitting next to her. He touched the hand resting on top of the comforter, buoyed when she didn't move it away. Her fingers curled around his trustingly. The vulnerability in the action was a shot to the heart. Even if she was angry with him, there was a part of her that trusted him instinctively to protect her.

And I'll always protect you, princess.

It was a vow that he'd carried since the day Rafe died and one he'd carry with him to the grave. But first he had to get her to eat.

"Baby, I brought you a tray. You need to eat something."

She immediately shook her head. "I'm not hungry."

Noah knelt next to the bed so she wouldn't have to crane her neck to see him. "Look, I know after the craziness of the last few days, you're coming down off that adrenaline high and aren't particularly hungry at the moment. And I know with the moving around you're having a hard time feeling safe. But I need you to keep your strength up. Try some of the fruit or maybe a piece of toast. Anything. Soup, you want soup? Can you do that for me?"

She slid him a glance that at least gave him some hope. It was a flicker of annoyance, but she sat up and scooted to the edge of the bed where he'd placed the tray. Lifting the spoon, she took exactly three sips of soup. Then she put the spoon down, gave him a pointed look, and scooted back to curl into a ball on the bed.

If Noah weren't so worried, he'd have laughed. That was the first hint he'd seen in a couple of days that his Lucia was in there somewhere. But he still needed her to eat, dammit. And more than three bites. But he knew how Lucia operated, and he couldn't force her to do anything she didn't want to. She'd only dig in her heels and hold out to spite him. People always thought he was the hardass, but they had no idea how stubborn one tiny little woman could be.

"Okay, fine. We'll try eating a little bit later."

This whole thing was completely fucked up. He'd almost lost the woman he loved, but even now that she was physically safe, she was gone. Or at least she was hiding and it didn't look like she had any intention of coming back soon. Luckily he had one more ace in the hole. He just hoped that Nonna would be able to get through to her. If this didn't work, he'd call in JJ. But JJ was a lot more difficult to control with all her questions and her suspicious nature.

"Lucia, I'm gonna need you to talk to me eventually. Tell me what's going on with you. We don't have to talk about it right now. But sooner or later we need to. You just take your time and rest for now."

At the door to the bedroom, Dylan gave a nod indicating that his surprise was here. Noah just hoped this was a good idea. He'd called Nonna and told her that there'd been a break in at the firm and while Lucia was fine, she could use a visit from her grandmother. It was all he'd really been able to tell her. What the fuck was he supposed to say? A homicidal maniac tried to kill Lucia the other day?

It wasn't an easy situation to explain.

Right now, he was down to a three-man crew. Him, Ryan and Dylan. Everyone else was still recovering. Oskar had a hell of a concussion. Jonas could still barely see. And Matthias, well, he was all kinds of fucked up. His pretty boy face would heal soon enough, but Noah owed the kid a debt he could never repay. He'd stopped that sonofabitch from taking Lucia at great personal cost. He'd always carry the scars from fending off that guy.

Considering the kind of hits he'd taken, he should be dead, but the kid would recover physically. He'd only ended up such a mess because he'd fought someone better trained, which was damn near impossible since Matthias had been trained by some of the best. Noah hated to think of the kind of monster Matthias had been forced to let out of his cage in order to protect Lucia. Was the killer here to stay now? Noah couldn't ask him, because unfortunately, the kid was another one who wasn't talking.

Granted a temporarily wired jaw would do that to you.

He strode out into the living room and nodded thanks to Ryan for picking up Nonna before he turned to the woman who was the only other person besides Lucia that he considered family.

"Nonna, good to see you."

She gave him a brief hug, and then pulled back. Her dark eyes searched his. "Where is Lucia? What on earth happened?"

He nodded and patted her shoulders. "Come with me. Lucia is in the bedroom. She's fine, just resting. I think it would be good for her to see you."

Nonna followed him, hesitating before she spoke. "Noah, you know I don't ask questions. But was Lucia … hurt?"

He knew what she meant immediately. "No, not like that."

Her shoulders dropped in relief. "Oh thank heavens. I didn't know what to think when you called."

Noah sighed, mentally working through what he could tell her. "There was a break in. My men were there. Someone tried to abduct her."

Nonna gasped and clutched her hand to her chest as she muttered a prayer. When she opened her eyes, Noah squeezed her hand to reassure her.

"She wasn't hurt physically, except for some scrapes and cuts. She's fine. I just think it would be good for her to see you."

Lucia was the only person the older woman had left of her family, so he felt like even more of an asshole to drop this kind of news on her so suddenly.

"She's in there."

Noah hung back as Nonna tiptoed into the bedroom. Lucia turned her head, then her eyebrows rose when she saw who it was. She pushed herself to a sitting position and her grandmother wrapped her arms around her, all the while whispering softly to her. Lucia started sobbing immediately, clinging to her grandmother like she was the only thing keeping her afloat. Seeing her so undone almost broke Noah completely. He should have called her grandmother immediately; she'd obviously needed the kind of comfort that only the woman who'd raised her could give.

But it was what Lucia said next that tore through him. "Nonna, I saw him. It was Rafe. He was here."

What the hell?

Noah left Lucia with her grandmother and staggered out into the hallway. He took a moment to lean against the wall, trying to make sense of what she'd just said. Did she really think that the man who'd been here was Rafe?

The anguish in her voice made it even worse. No wonder Lucia wasn't talking to him. She'd hardly talk about her beloved brother with the man responsible for his death. He was suddenly overwhelmed by everything that had happened and all of the emotions tangled up in it. Noah pressed his hands over his eyes, as if he could hold in the guilt and his own grief by pure force.

"I did this to her," he whispered out loud.

The guilt of it hit him so hard he almost dropped to his knees. He'd made the mistake of thinking that Lucia was fine after the trauma of seeing her brother shot in front of her. Nonna always said Lucia was her rock during that time. They'd commended her on being so strong and moving past it when clearly she'd been struggling this whole time. They'd been happy to assume she was fine because it meant they didn't have to worry about her anymore. They'd failed her. Especially him. Because he knew more than anyone just how traumatic the experience had actually been.

He contemplated getting his things and leaving. The other guys could protect her, and she wouldn't have to see him again. It couldn't be good for her having to look at the man responsible for the single most traumatic event in her life every day. He was the cause and root of the very thing haunting her. Even as he had the thought, he knew he couldn't leave. Even with a houseful of guys watching her, she'd still almost been taken. It wasn't hubris to think that he was the best man to protect her. He'd been a top operative with ORUS for a reason, and it wasn't because the big bosses had wanted to throw him a bone. He had been one of the best because he'd been trained by one of the best. He might be the last person Lucia wanted to see, but he was still her best shot at survival.

No matter what, he'd help her. She needed to talk to someone. Blake Security didn't have a shrink on call, but he'd find the best. After all, it was only money. He had more than he would ever need of that. She was his and always had been. The love of his life. He had to protect her no matter what.

He knew the anniversary of her brother's death had messed with her for years. But this? She seriously thought she had seen Rafe? Maybe he should have been more up-front with her. Or maybe he'd been *too* honest? Maybe she hadn't been ready to hear the truth about her brother and what they'd done.

No one wanted to hear that someone they loved was a killer. An assassin. He'd get her the help. His Lucia was in there somewhere. He just had to help her find a way out.

With a deep inhale, he pushed away from the wall and strode down the hall to check on the rest of his men. They'd turned the master bedroom into a temporary sick bay with three smaller beds. Dr. Breckner was checking Jonas's sight.

"How are we doing, Doc?"

"He's improving every day. But whatever that substance was, I think I have a hit." The doctor left Jonas's side and went over to his computer. "When I tested the sample of what was in his eyes, I found traces of what appears to be a synthetic toxin. I've never seen anything like it, especially in aerosol form. The properties of this particular compound attack the optic nerve. But he seems to be recovering, which is remarkable. It's as though the effects are only meant to be temporary. I plan on spending the rest of the afternoon digging through literature to see if I can find anything like it."

Fucking hell. Noah sighed.

"Don't bother. I know what that stuff is. There's an antidote. I have a contact; he can get you some." And Ian had better fucking come through for him.

The doctor blinked at him. "You know what this is? Where does it come from?"

Noah shifted on his feet under the scrutiny of the doctor. He didn't want to tell the guy too much and get him killed. But then again, he was an on-call doctor for plenty of shady types. He probably did other things worthy of getting killed.

"It comes from the Himalayas. The aerosol is derived from a plant. Once I get my hands on the antidote, I'll let you know. I need Jonas back on his feet as soon as possible."

"But that's impossible. His vision is getting better, but healing takes time. Even a month is an optimistic estimate, and two is more likely."

Noah squared his shoulders. They didn't have a month. Jonas was one of his best. Hell, they needed all hands on deck. They were going after that asshole.

"Trust me, Doc. I'll get it to you later today."

That was the least Ian could do. Yeah, his old friend had alerted him, but he'd still done nothing to stop it. *You know that's not how it works.*

Noah ground his teeth. Yeah, he understood how ORUS worked. Once a hit went out, there was no way to stop it. And any interference by any agent would result in immediate termination—the hard way. But still, Noah hated it. Hated that he'd almost lost. Hated that it was his past that almost cost him the woman he loved.

Ian at least owed him that antidote. And when this was over, they were having a conversation about exactly how ORUS was run and who was steering the boat. Because if he had to, Noah would dismantle the whole organization brick by brick, man by man. It wouldn't be easy, but if anything happened to Lucia, that would be his new life's goal.

The doctor looked skeptical, but he nodded. "I know better than to ask questions. But your man, he's still my patient. I want to run some tests on whatever you bring me before I use it."

Noah sighed. "Fine. But you'll find out just what I told you. It'll work. And it'll put Jonas back on his feet in a couple of days, not months. What about Matthias and Oskar?"

Dr. Breckner consulted another chart. "Matthias is healing well. He won't need reconstructive surgery. And he isn't likely to scar. He no longer has a concussion. But emotionally, like your girlfriend, he's not responsive. Answers questions when asked, but otherwise he's not talking."

Noah felt like a hand was squeezing around his heart. Matthias needed him, but he couldn't take the time out to deal with that right now. They were under attack.

"And Oskar?"

"He'll need another few days. His concussion was more severe than Matthias's. The arm was dislocated, but nothing was broken, so give him a couple weeks and he'll be back to one hundred percent."

"Thanks, doc. I appreciate you coming on short notice."

Dr. Breckner nodded. "Of course. We go way back, Noah. You call, I come."

Noah nodded his thanks again and went to find Dylan for a status update on the penthouse. He found him messing with the security monitors.

"Everything look okay?"

Dylan grunted. "I'm decent with these things but I'm no Matthias."

"I hear you. The kid's gonna be on his feet soon enough, so you'll only have to play tech-support for a while. What's the status on the old penthouse?"

"I got to the place before the police showed up. There was a body on the fourteenth floor. Dressed in all black, ski mask. Dead. Looked like he'd been that way for a while. Thing was, there was no blood on him. Cause of death was probably a pinprick found in the base of his neck. Poison of some sort, I think. But it clearly wasn't the guy the rest of the team fought."

Noah frowned. "They sent two of them? What the hell? Did one of them kill the other?"

It made no sense.

Dylan shrugged and continued. "I took care of the body. Took it to the incinerator down at the morgue. I wasn't seen."

Noah nodded. "Thanks."

Dylan shifted on his feet. "Boss, there was something else."

Noah lifted a brow. "Yeah?"

"He had tattoos on him. On each of his wrists, on his back, and his feet. At first, they looked like random freckles or dots. But when I looked closer, they looked like stars. I took a picture and then plugged it into a search engine. I was right. It was a tattoo of the constellation Aries."

"Aries?" Noah hoped his voice was even. He'd known the body would have the signature markings. What he didn't anticipate was Dylan finding out.

Dylan nodded. "Yeah. I noticed it looks similar to the ones you and Matthias have. Yours is Leo. Matthias's, I'm not sure."

Noah pinned an intense stare on Dylan. "You don't want to open that particular Pandora's box."

Dylan backed off. "Yep. I know better. Just saying. Whatever you guys are into, or whatever's coming back to bite you in the ass, we're a team. I just want to know, are they coming for you, or are they coming for her?"

Noah crossed his arms and met the other man's dark stare. "They're coming for all of us."

Chapter Three

Lucia woke up with the beginnings of a scream in her throat. She panted for a few seconds as the tendrils of the dream slid from her mind. She rolled over, confused when her eyes landed on bare brick walls. Then she blinked and it all came back. The attack. Moving to a new place.

Rafe.

She'd been dreaming about that day in the car with Rafe. It was bothering her that she couldn't remember what he'd done right before leaving. What had he been doing at the back of the car for so long?

Lulu.

That voice was going to haunt her until she figured it out. There were so many different explanations for what she'd heard. Maybe it was someone she'd known as a child. Her nickname had been used more then. Although she couldn't imagine someone holding a grudge that long. Why come back and hurt her now? It could have been the result of all this stress, causing her to imagine things. But then why had the guy tensed when she'd said Rafe's name?

She hadn't imagined that part, she was sure of it.

The futility of it all was maddening. But this wasn't going to paralyze her. She was determined to do something productive.

After pulling on a tank top and shorts, she walked out to the main area. Oskar sat on the couch watching TV, the sling on his arm not detracting from his incredibly ripped bare chest.

Sweet Lord.

These guys were enough to give a woman a heart attack. She'd always been Noah's through and through, but she wasn't dead. Any woman with a pulse would take a second look at a man who looked like Oskar when he was shirtless. She giggled. Even Nonna would probably take a second look, although she'd no doubt say a Hail Mary afterward.

"Morning, Oskar. Have you seen Noah?"

He inclined his head toward the hallway. "He's been in there with Matthias for a while. You need something?"

Her heart flipped over as warmth spread through her body. She really was the luckiest girl in the world. These guys would do anything for her, including give their lives to protect her. She walked closer and put a gentle hand on his shoulder right above where the sling started.

"I should be asking you that. How is your arm?"

He shrugged. "It's still attached. What more can I ask for?"

Lucia couldn't resist a grin. He really was too much sometimes. Big, brutal and aggressive, but then he'd turn around and do something sweet out of the blue. Whatever girl caught his eye was going to have her hands full not falling head over heels for the big lug.

"Do you want breakfast? Although I just realized we probably don't have any food here."

"You're cooking? Oh thank you, thank you. I'll be a good boy Mommy if you just make me pancakes." Oskar leaned his head against her arm and softened his gorgeous face into a pitiful mask. It was all the more amusing since he was such a huge, aggressive-looking guy.

"Pancakes? I'm thinking we'll be lucky to find cold cereal in this place."

"Noah had a huge order of groceries delivered earlier. So there's hopefully something decent in there. I'm ready to eat cardboard at this point."

Lucia stroked his hair affectionately, unable to resist a little tenderness. "That won't be necessary. I'll find something."

She walked into the kitchen and discovered that Oskar hadn't exaggerated when he said the order was huge. The pantry was filled until there was almost no space left and the refrigerator looked just as packed. Since all the guys were hanging around it made sense though. This food would no doubt be gone in just a few days.

Unashamed

Her phone vibrated in her pocket, and she answered it absently while sifting through the contents in the pantry.

"Lucia! Thank God. I just heard what happened. Are you okay?" JJ's voice was just shy of hysterical.

When she finally found the pancake mix, she put it on the counter and then started looking through the refrigerator for milk and eggs. It took a while since she had to shift stuff around to see what was in the back.

"Sorry, I was going to call you today. Things have just been so crazy. Wait, how did you find out?"

"Adriana told us that your boyfriend called in for you. Said your apartment had been vandalized and you'd need a few days off."

"Noah called. Of course he did. That's not exactly what happened though."

As she filled JJ in on everything that had happened, she mixed the pancakes and started frying them in a pan she found in one of the lower cabinets. She ended with, "So Noah showed up just in time before the guy could get me out the window. I think that thing he put around my waist was some kind of harness. Otherwise, I'm not sure how he planned to get down the side of the building carrying me but I guess kidnappers aren't that smart."

37

JJ huffed out a laugh. "Either that or he was planning to tie you to his back first. Maybe he's not used to stealing people. He's probably used to snatching laptops or something."

Lucia thought back to how the man in black had held off Oskar, Jonas and Matthias simultaneously. She shivered. This was no garden-variety purse snatcher. He was more like Superman. Just her luck to attract a near-invincible psycho stalker.

Once she had a nice stack of pancakes, she made a plate for Oskar and brought it to him in the main area along with an unopened container of pancake syrup and a fork. The look of adulation on his face made her laugh all over again.

"The moment Noah fucks up, I'm taking his place. I don't need much. Just keep feeding me like this." Oskar speared a huge hunk of pancake with the fork and took an obnoxiously large bite.

"Be a good boy and I'll make you some bacon, too."

"I love you. Please leave Noah's cranky ass and marry me. I may not be as pretty but baby I've got everything else you need."

"Whose sexy voice is that?" JJ demanded. "And why do you have all the hotties breathing on you lately?

Share the love, please!"

Lucia laughed. "It's just Oskar being silly." She turned to Oskar. "Don't let Noah hear you say that or he'll dislocate the other arm."

Oskar rolled his eyes but then turned his concentration to working the fork left-handed. She left him with his exaggerated moans and groans of enjoyment and went back to the counter to eat her own food.

"Well, I'm glad that you're okay."

Lucia was quiet, unsure if she wanted to tell JJ the whole truth. But as usual her best friend could sense when she was holding out.

"Are you really okay, Lucia? Things have been pretty intense lately. Anybody would be freaked out."

"I *am* freaked out. Especially since the guy who was here … JJ he had my brother's voice. I swear, it sounded just like Rafe."

JJ didn't respond and she could practically feel her friend's concern coming through the phone. "Lucia …"

"I know what you're going to say. It sounds crazy, believe me I know. But when I said his name he froze, like he wasn't sure what to do. And he called me Lulu. No one calls me that anymore, not even Nonna."

"That's … okay I'm not going to pretend I can explain it, but that doesn't mean it's Rafe. People don't just disappear for years with no trace. Why would he even want to do that?"

"People fake their deaths," Lucia protested.

"Yeah, in the *movies*. Or people with shitty lives they want to escape. Or tax evaders. None of which applies to Rafe. Your brother would have never left you and Nonna to fend for yourselves. He adored you."

Lucia hung her head. It made her feel disloyal to have even thought it when she knew that JJ was right. Her brother would have never just disappeared with no word no matter how bad things were in his life. Rafe had been many things but never a coward. He would have faced bullets head on before leaving her and Nonna alone in the world. But that voice… She couldn't just let this go when the sound of her brother's voice was still echoing in her ear.

"It sounded just like him. Don't I owe it to him to at least investigate?"

"How? There really isn't anything you can do. I hate to point out the obvious sweetie but we have no resources to handle something like this."

Lucia smiled. "Actually that's not true. I have the best resource of all. My memories. I know Rafe. What he liked, what was important to him. If he really is alive, then he's still the same person and as much as he might try to disguise himself, there are some things you can't change."

JJ sighed. Lucia knew that her friend was trying to be supportive but didn't really believe her.

"Just say it. I know you think this is crazy."

"I think you're distraught and grasping onto anything that can bring you comfort. I understand that. What worries me is that you seem convinced already that he's alive. I don't want you to get hurt, that's all."

"You're worried about me, I know. But I'll be careful, I promise."

After talking about a few random things happening in the office, they hung up with Lucia promising to keep JJ in the loop about what was going on. The whole time in the back of her mind she was turning over ideas. How did you smoke out a person who was hiding from everyone?

By the time she finished cleaning the kitchen, she had a plan.

Lucia didn't have the opportunity to put her plan into action until the next week. It had taken her that long to figure out how to get Noah's help. She couldn't just ask him for it straight out because he'd think it was weird and probably just keep pushing her to talk to a shrink. It was so irritating the way he assumed he always knew best.

Lucia rolled her eyes. She'd long ago learned that the best way to handle these alpha-male types of guys was to let them think everything was their idea. Rafe had been the same way and she'd been a master at handling him before she even hit her teen years.

Thinking about Rafe brought her mind back to what she was doing. She looked out the window at the scenery flashing by as they raced over the highway.

It was a beautiful day for an adventure. At least that was how Lucia had posed the idea of visiting the clock tower at the state library in Connecticut. It had been her mother's favorite place in the world, and she'd taken Rafe and Lucia there often before she died.

After their mother's death, Rafe would bring her there whenever she was sad or lonely. When the girls at school picked on her for wearing secondhand clothes or for her wild bushy hair, he'd pick her up from school early and they'd go sit in the courtyard behind the library and look up at the clock tower. She used to pretend that if she stared hard enough she could make the hands of the clock turn faster or even go backward. That she was in control of all the bad things that happened and could fix them whenever she wanted. Even after she was old enough to recognize just how powerless she was in the world, it had brought her comfort to see it.

Rafe had never had much imagination, so he'd sit and eat sunflower seeds while she hummed to herself, lost in her daydreams. He'd been patient that way, not needing to say or do anything, content to just let her dream. She'd often wondered how he could do that, just sit and wait without moving a muscle, but he'd never rushed her or made her feel like he'd rather be somewhere else.

Her brother had always made her feel like she was the most important person in his life. Maybe that was why none of her boyfriends had ever had a chance, even if they'd been able to get past Noah. Rafe had taught her early how she should be treated by a man and Lucia wasn't willing to settle for less. Even in death, her brother's shoes were hard to fill. She'd always known it would take a hell of a man to even come close.

And I did come pretty close, she thought as she looked

over at Noah. His fingers were sure on the steering wheel and his profile was tight with tension but he hadn't tried to talk her out of coming here. When she'd explained that she needed to go somewhere familiar, somewhere she could remember the good times with her family, he just nodded and got to work making it happen.

Was it any wonder she loved him so completely? Even when he made her crazy, she couldn't deny he did it all because he thought it was for her own good.

They pulled off the highway and Noah finally spoke. "Ryan is following us and will observe from a distance. I'd like to keep our visit to less than an hour if possible. I want you to have your time, you know that, but I can't put you at risk." He glanced at her warily as if worried she'd be pissed about the restrictions.

"I understand. Thanks for making this happen for me. I'm sure you'd rather keep me at home under lock and key."

Noah snorted but at least there was a smile on his face now. "I'd bubble wrap you and put you behind glass if I could."

Lucia didn't doubt it. "Let's pass on that. It'd be hard to cuddle if I was in bubble wrap. And other things." She leaned over and cupped him between his legs, insanely turned on by his deep groan.

"*Christ*, are you trying to make me crash this car?"
He gently removed her hand but kissed her fingers before
releasing them. "What happened to my innocent little
princess?"

"You corrupted her and she decided she liked being
bad."

She was teasing but even as she said it, Lucia
realized it was true. Being with Noah had opened her up in
so many ways and she loved feeling so confident and safe to
explore with him.

She was quiet the rest of the way and didn't even
notice how much time had passed until Noah turned the car
off. The parking lot was mainly empty since it was the
middle of a weekday. Noah got out first, looking around the
car with a shrewd eye and a harsh expression. Anyone who
wanted to screw with them would be crazy to try anything
while he looked like that. Later, she'd be sure to tell him just
how arousing she found that harsh, unyielding expression.
Maybe she'd whisper it while he was inside her just to drive
him crazy.

She smiled at the thought.

When he opened her door, Lucia accepted his hand

to get down and then followed as he led her toward the library. They walked inside and Lucia looked around, anxious to see if it looked different to her after so many years away. The far left wall had been converted to a row of computer stations which was new; it had previously been the periodical section. The carpet was a different color and she didn't recognize the librarians behind the counter. Other than that, it looked much the same. Warmth flowed through her at the familiar sights that used to represent family and comfort.

Access to the courtyard and the clock tower was through the back door, so they walked across the main floor. Lucia grinned at a small group of toddlers huddled around a librarian reading in an animated voice. When she was younger, she'd imagined that one day when she grew up and got married she'd bring her own children here for story time. It had been so long since she'd thought of that. Of course, that was before everything in her life changed so dramatically. After Rafe's death, she no longer dreamed of weddings and princes to sweep her off her feet.

Not when she'd gotten the most definitive proof of all that fairy tales were just that, tales. Real life was never so neat.

They stepped onto the back patio and followed the

path leading to the clock tower. Lucia gazed up at it, still awed by how majestic it seemed. She turned in a slow circle, noting the neat landscaping of small shrubs and flowers around the base of the tower. The color of the red brick had faded slightly over the years, but it was obvious that it was clean and well cared for.

"It looks the same," she whispered.

She wasn't sure what she'd expected. For it to look as weathered and tired as she felt on the inside, perhaps? But no, it looked solid and strong, exactly as it had always been. The only thing that had changed was her. While her world had been shattered, the rest of the world had kept on spinning.

"You're crying," Noah stated, looking completely lost.

Lucia raised a hand to her face and was startled to see the moisture on her fingers. She was in fact crying.

"What's wrong, Lulu?"

His use of her nickname just made it worse somehow, reminding her of days long gone and a time that she could never recapture. She'd never again be that girl who believed in the impossible and only had to look to her brother leaning against the tower to feel centered again.

What had she really hoped to accomplish coming here? Had she thought that Rafe would coincidentally be there and pop out saying 'Surprise' or something? It was ridiculous that she'd allowed herself to get excited about yet another fairy tale that couldn't come true.

"Let's go. I've seen enough."

"Okay, whatever you want." Noah watched her with a worried look on his face. No doubt he wanted to ask why she'd wanted him to drive her all the way out here only to cry and then leave after two minutes. She was glad he didn't ask because she had no answers to give him.

She walked to the base of the tower and put one hand on the cool brick. The rough texture under her hands made it real somehow. This was the last time she'd ever come here. It was too painful to look back at the past knowing what she'd lost.

"Goodbye Rafe," she whispered.

Then she saw it. At the base of the clock tower.

Sunflower seeds.

Chapter Four

Noah watched as Lucia moved to the base of the clock tower and leaned against it. He never should have brought her here. This was bringing up bad memories, obviously, since she was already crying. He moved closer, intending to pull her away when she suddenly smiled.

This was the first time Noah had seen Lucia smile in ages. Her *real* smile, not the strained version she'd had pasted on for the last week. What the hell was going on?

"You okay, sweetheart?"

She grinned up at him. "I'm perfect. Thank you for bringing me up here. I missed this. Missed that sense of home."

She shivered a little. The hot and sticky July had given way to an even hotter and stickier August for the most part. But from up here, the breeze coming in from over the ocean hit them just right, making it much cooler up here at the clock tower.

Lucia wrapped her arms around his neck. "I love you, Noah."

Automatically, his arms wrapped around her, holding her in the shelter of his embrace. Jesus, he'd missed this. He'd missed *her*. Her smile, her laugh and even her shouting. "I love you too."

She rose on her tiptoes to press a soft kiss against his

lips. But this was different from the brief, chaste kisses she'd been giving him for the last week or so. This kiss lingered. Just like in the car, he was taken off guard. Noah wanted her so badly, but he didn't want to push her too fast or pressure her. He needed to let her drive.

Waiting to see what it was that she needed, he kissed her gently, letting her take the lead. It went against every fiber in his body to do so, but he could do it. *Do it for her*.

She pulled back with a frown. "Noah, why aren't you kissing me?"

"I thought that's what we were just doing, princess."

She shook her head. "No, that's not how you kiss me. When you kiss me, it drowns everything out. And all I can think about is you, and me, and us, and getting naked as quickly as possible."

Oh, yeah; real helpful. She just had to go and say the naked word. One word from her and his dick was ready to play. The blood rushed to his cock like the damn thing was on fire.

"Sweetheart, you've been through a lot. So maybe we should take it slow?"

Lucia gave him a coquettish smile that told him she

knew exactly what she was doing to him. "And if I don't want to take it slow?"

Noah licked his lips. What was she playing at? What the hell was going on with her? At the same time, all he wanted to do was nuzzle her, inhale her scent, and see if he could get her to make that sound at the back of her throat that she always did when she was about to come. He was desperate to hear it again. But he knew something was off.

"Sweetheart, you know how much I love you. And you know how much I miss you." Lucia pressed against him and they both moaned. "You can feel how much I've missed you. But I want to make sure you're doing okay before we move forward. I don't want you to retreat from me again. It scared the shit out of me."

"I'm not retreating. I just know what I want. I've missed you. Everything was a shock and I didn't know how to deal, but now I've sorted it all out. Coming here, coming home in essence, it's making me better. I just want you to help me feel better. Feel more alive, more like myself." She rocked her hips slightly, and Noah swore he saw stars.

"Lucia —"

She nuzzled into his throat, her lips softly teasing and playing over his Adam's apple. "Noah—" she mimicked his tone.

Unashamed

"Sweetheart, this is not the best —"

She cut him off effectively by delving her hand into his jeans and wrapping her delicate hand around his erection.

Oh shit. It was as if all higher brain processing had been turned off, all functioning ceased. Lucia snapped open the top button of his jeans, and the *zick-zick-zick* as the zipper went down only ratcheted his arousal even higher. She had him out of the confines of his jeans and boxers in seconds.

"Lucia. This isn't a good idea. Anyone could see us up here."

"So what if anyone sees us? I need the man I love inside of me right now. I don't want to wait. I don't want to go back home. I want to enjoy the view. I want to dig my nails into your back as you slide into me. I want to feel alive, Noah. Help me feel alive."

Her words tore through him. He knew what he should do. He knew what would probably be better for her. The problem was, that knowledge was somewhere way in the recesses of his mind. Because, well, he was a guy, and she had her hand on his dick. So that meant he didn't have two brain cells to rub together at the moment, let alone the cognitive willpower to stop this.

"Sweetheart. I love the way you do that."

Fuck, did he love it. Her hands were so soft and warm. And they certainly felt better than him making good use of his right hand in the shower every morning. But he had to at least try to be the reasonable one.

"Let's at least go back—"

She squeezed him and his knees buckled. "I told you, I don't want to go to the car. I'm ready here. I'm wet, Noah. You want to feel how much?"

All thinking stopped. All he knew at that moment was he needed to be inside her. Needed to feel her warmth and her slick heat as she wrapped around his dick, squeezing, pulsing, and milking him. Her dress rode up. And his hands slid up her knees, widening her thighs the farther he went. With his thumbs, he traced the edge of her panties, and Lucia threw her head back.

"Oh God, Noah."

Hearing her moaning his name, all low and sultry like that, made him jerk. The only thoughts his brain offered were, *Inside. Now. Need.* Yeah, full sentences were so not his thing at the moment. She was wet. So fucking wet. Both thumbs snuck past the edge of her panties, one went straight to her clit, gently smoothing over it, as he dipped his head and took her mouth. As he kissed her deep, licking into the warmth between her lips, his other thumb found her wet center and slid in easily. She rocked her hips into his hands, questing, searching.

God, he needed this. *They* needed this. Maybe they could find their way back to each other if he could just wrap himself around her, hold her tight and keep her safe. And keep her loved. If he kept her loved, they'd both be able to stop worrying.

Lucia was impatient. With her hands, she shoved at his jeans, pushing them down over his hips and his ass.

With a curse, Noah drew back, hooked his whole hand into her soaking panties, and tugged. The ripping sound barely registered as it mixed with the sound of her panting and his groan. In seconds, his cock was nudging her slick entrance. He held the base tightly and gently rubbed against her. Covered himself with her slick juices. Shit. So fucking good. She was so wet. So ready.

"Noah. Please. I need—"

She didn't have to ask twice. He slammed home.

Lucia tossed her head back, exposing her throat. He leaned over to brush his lips along the column of her neck and sucked gently. Even as one hand scooped under her ass to keep her stationary as he made love to her, the cold of the unyielding stone against his arms made him flinch but he didn't care. All he wanted was to drive home. To keep feeling her slick heat tightening around him. Fuck, how had he lasted for more than a few hours, let alone days without this?

Lucia shoved her hands in his hair and held him to her. With a frustrated groan, she yanked at her clothes, struggling to tug down the strap of her sundress.

Against her neck he whispered, "You want my mouth on you? You want me to suck your nipples?"

"Yes, Noah. God, yes."

He shifted her up and back until her head and shoulders were just off of the stone platform, giving him the angle he needed to dip his head and take her into his mouth. The moment he did, she moaned low and her inner walls tightened around him. He switched to her other breast, sucking her through the thin material and fabric, while his thumb teased her other nipple, pinching lightly. All the while, he drove deep, claiming her once again as his. His cock sliding and retreating, sliding and retreating. Every time he bottomed out, she made this low keening sound at the back of her throat like she'd just discovered bliss.

And then he felt it. Her hands tightened in his hair, and she held him to her breasts as she screamed out, "Oh, my God, Noah. Yes, right there. Right there. Right—" Her climax crashed into her, and her whole body locked around his like a vise. She was never letting him go.

"Oh shit. *Fuuuck, Lucia.*" With three quick jerks, he was following her. Their climaxes mingled so that he couldn't tell where one of them ended and the other one began. Exactly the way it should be.

"I love you," he whispered.

"And I love you, Noah Blake."

An hour later, Lucia stood in the shower and let the hot spray pelt her skin. Had they really just done that? The blush on her cheeks mingled with the hot water.

Public sex.

She'd never done anything like that in her life and as reckless as it had been, she couldn't bring herself to regret any of it. She could still feel Noah's hands gripping her hips. The bruising sting of his kiss. He'd been completely out of control, and she'd loved every minute of it.

She'd certainly taken him off guard. Truthfully, she had taken herself off guard. But considering what she'd seen that day, a little uncharacteristic behavior was to be expected. It had been such a shock to see those sunflower seeds there. Despite what she'd told JJ, she hadn't actually thought she'd find any evidence of Rafe just by haunting the places they'd used to go. But this was something she couldn't ignore. Anyone else would think she was insane, but she just *knew* how those seeds had gotten there. And they'd looked fresh. He'd been there. Recently. Rafe was alive.

Or you're crazy.

She let the thought slide over her, turning it over in her head. Maybe she was crazy. Maybe she was seeing things that weren't there. Her behavior up in that clock tower was reckless at best. Everything she'd done lately was reckless and out of character. The only thing her digging had accomplished so far was to get her nearly killed, more than once. Not to mention the danger all of her friends were in because of her. Matthias, Jonas, and Oskar were going to be suffering for weeks because of her. All of this was because she was asking questions ... about Rafe.

She didn't want to think she was losing it. She'd heard his voice. *But you didn't see his face.* No, she hadn't. But it was possible.

Unashamed

The memories had been coming back a little more every day. She remembered so much more about what had happened before the gunshot that changed everything. When Rafe had gone around the back of the car, he'd taken his shirt off and put on something else, then put the shirt back on. Was it possible that he'd been putting on a bulletproof vest? There was no way to know for sure, but the fact that it was possible was just one more puzzle piece in a jumble of others that she had to make sense of. But no matter how she spun things, it was possible that he was alive.

But, if he was alive, then what was he doing? Why was he trying to hurt her?

He hasn't actually tried to kill you.

Maybe they had been looking at everything the wrong way. Had he just been trying to take her? Why? And where the hell had he been all this time? She leaned against the wall and tried to drown out the doubt and worry.

Noah knocked on the bathroom door. "Hey, princess? You locked the door. How am I supposed to join you if you lock me out?"

Lucia knew full well if he wanted in, he'd just take the damn door off the hinges. But he was giving her some semblance of privacy. "Sorry, I just needed a few."

And man did she. Her shoulders, her hips, and her ass were all abraded thanks to that stone platform Noah had put her on to screw her senseless. *No, that wasn't his fault; that was yours.* She'd just been so happy to find those sunflower seeds. So happy to know that maybe she wasn't crazy, she'd wanted to celebrate. She'd wanted to feel Noah.

"You can come in," she called out.

"Okay, give me a minute. I'm just going to check in with Jonas so we won't be interrupted."

Lucia smiled at that. She figured he was trying to make her laugh by mentioning the other guys' tendency to interrupt or walk in on them accidently.

He was trying so hard, but no matter what she did she couldn't claw herself out from the darkness. She just kept hearing Rafe's voice over and over again. All these years later, clear as day. Calling her Lulu. And of course every time she looked at Noah, she saw Rafe. So that made things worse.

But now, now that he might be alive? She needed to find out. Where he'd been, what he had been doing, why he left her, left Nonna. It wasn't going to solve everything, but at least if she could get some proof she wouldn't have to see that look on everyone's faces. The look that said they thought she was losing her mind but were too polite to mention it. Maybe they all thought this was just an overdue breakdown that she should have had right after her brother's death.

The only person who was fully in her corner was half-crazy herself. JJ was always ready to run in like a crusader. Maybe in this instance that made JJ a little off her rocker.

But what if you're right? What if it was Rafe? That was the thought that dragged her out of the darkness. If her brother was alive, she was going to find him. Even if she knew everyone else would think it was crazy.

The slap of cold air on her backside brought her out of her thoughts. She hadn't even heard Noah unlock the door.

"Is everything okay? You've been in here for a while." He picked up the loofah sponge that she'd been using and dragged it gently over her arms and then down her back.

Lucia smiled up at him. "Just thinking about everything. Plus the hot water was helping soothe all the muscles I strained while having sex against a brick tower. Remind me not to do that again."

Noah's hands followed the path of the sponge. The

gentle touch sent shivers up and down her spine. She closed her eyes and enjoyed the sensation of being warm and naked with him.

"I would point out that I tried to be responsible and stop things. But I was forced by a saucy vixen to do dirty things in public against my better judgment."

Lucia raised an eyebrow. "Against your will, huh?"

"Well, you were saying dirty things like *I need you inside me, Noah* and *I'm so wet for you, Noah*. What red-blooded man could resist that? There is no willpower in the world that could withstand that kind of sorcery."

She chuckled at his disgruntled expression. "Does that mean you don't want me to use my witchy powers on you again? Because I could leave you to shower alone. But that would be a shame because I really wanted to taste this."

He sucked in a hard breath when her hands circled him, tugging on his hard length and playing with the soft skin of the head.

"Oh, you should definitely do what you want to do. I'm already under your spell after all. What's one more thing?"

Lucia nodded her head slowly and then sank to her knees before him. His eyes got dark as he watched her greedily. She took him in her mouth, happy to lose herself in bringing pleasure to her man instead of worrying about things she couldn't control.

Chapter Five

Noah knocked on Nonna's front door. It occurred
to him that he probably should have called first but as soon

as he'd had the idea, his feet had started moving. Honestly, he wasn't even sure what he was going to say. He was completely winging it here. Lucia would be pissed if she knew where he was, but he needed to talk to Nonna. He was *that* worried, and Lucia's grandmother was quite possibly the only one who could help.

Footsteps sounded inside and a second later the door opened. Nonna was wearing a beautiful rose-colored sweater and had her hair twisted back into a low bun. Although he knew objectively that she'd aged over the years, to him she would always be the same. Elegant. Angelic. One of the only people who'd looked at him and seen more than what was on the outside.

As usual, when she saw him she smiled like she was getting a visit from a celebrity. Noah grinned back, thinking as he always did how lucky he'd been that day that Rafe had dragged him here for dinner. Rafe had done more than mentor him; he'd saved him in every way that mattered. When a man got used to having a family that treated him like this, it was no wonder he'd lay down his life for them.

"Noah, come in. Don't just stand outside. I don't know why you don't use your key. You're family." She welcomed him with a hug and he stooped down slightly so she could kiss his cheek.

Her protestations made him smile, although he would never tell her why he didn't use his key. The friend he'd tasked to watch over Nonna had been strangely closemouthed about her activities over recent years, and Noah had a sneaking suspicion that it was because they were more than just friends. Noah didn't have any true family anymore. Nonna and Lucia were the closest things to it he had, so he valued them highly.

The last thing he needed was to walk in on his pseudo-grandmother in a compromising position. An unfortunate mental image popped into his mind, and he shut it down immediately. Noah shuddered. There were just some things you couldn't unsee.

"I never know where my key is, so it's just easier to knock," he lied, feeling no shame for it. If he believed in God, he was sure any benevolent being would forgive him an untruth under these circumstances.

He followed her into the interior of the house and instantly felt at home. It was a talent that Nonna DeMarco had, making visitors feel like family within seconds of entering her home. He glanced around at the old furniture and handmade throw blankets covering the back of the couch. Nonna DeMarco despised waste of any kind so everything in her home was either handmade or secondhand. It was the most comforting place he'd ever been in.

Not sure how to bring up the reason for his visit, Noah allowed her to fuss over him, making him a cup of coffee even though he'd already had some. By the time the coffee was ready, he'd had a chance to think about how he wanted to bring up Lucia's recent behavior in a way that wasn't going to alarm the older woman.

When they were settled on the couch, Nonna raised her eyebrows at him. If he'd been younger, it was the kind of look that would have made him think he was in trouble for something or other.

"What?"

"Just wondering when you're going to tell me the real reason why you're here. I know it's not just to visit."

Feeling like a little boy caught with his hand in the cookie jar, he smiled. "Maybe I just wanted to check on you."

"Hmm. You know I'm fine."

Noah sighed. There was no point in trying to ease her into it. Just like when they were young, Nonna had radar for when one of her 'children' needed something. "You're right. I'm not just here to chat. It's Lucia. She isn't doing well."

Immediately Nonna's face lost its teasing smile. "She's been through so much. I think the stress is finally catching up with her."

Noah didn't want to voice his true thoughts, that this was so much worse than stress. Lucia had lost all grip on reality. After days of wondering what was going on with her, she'd finally confessed why she'd asked to go to the clock tower and what she'd found there. She was convinced her brother was alive, which didn't make any sense considering that she'd watched him get shot. Noah had shot him point blank. He'd searched for a pulse before taking Lucia away to safety.

There was no one outside of Lucia or Nonna who wanted Rafe to be alive more than he did, but it just wasn't possible. Her insistence on something she *knew* to be impossible worried him more than anything else could have.

"Give her time." Nonna's softly creased face bore the signs of her worry for her granddaughter.

He hated to drop all this in her lap and cause her worry, but he truly didn't know who else to talk to about this. No one else understood their situation, and she was also the only person he believed could get through to Lucia. Nonna could make her see that pursuing this was just asking for more heartbreak. She was the only one on the face of the planet who loved Lucia as much as he did. He knew how much she'd sacrificed to take in Rafe and Lucia after their parents' death.

"I've given her time. Maybe too much time."

Maybe he'd been a fool to think that they could just move past it once she remembered their traumatic shared past. Watching the man you love shoot your brother wasn't the kind of thing one could just get over. Lucia likely needed more therapy. A lot more. Not that he could convince her of that.

The whole thing was a fucking mess.

"There's no such thing as too much time when mourning a lost family member," Nonna murmured. "I'm still not over losing Luca."

Noah could understand what she meant, but he feared that he'd already done too much of that. The way he felt about Lucia was dangerous. He would forgive her anything, and he was worried that his love for her blinded him to serious issues. If she really needed help, he wanted to make sure she got it. There was a very real danger that he'd bury his head in the sand because he didn't want to admit that she needed help.

For her sake, he had to be stronger than that.

Apparently his thoughts were evident on his face because Nonna reached over and grabbed his hands. He startled but forced himself not to jerk back. Noah wasn't used to physical contact. Usually when he got this close to someone, it was because he was about to take their life. But when Nonna touched him, all the stress and pain of the last few days hit him at once. Her fingers curled around his and Noah had to avert his gaze, afraid he was going to cry like a baby at the show of tenderness.

"Noah, I know you don't understand yet, but women are different. Lucia is like me, strong on the outside but she is *dolce*, sweet and soft, on the inside. There were times right after Rafe's death when I wasn't able to accept that he was gone. I would catch a glimpse of a man on the street and be convinced it was him. I would hear a voice in a crowd and follow it, sure it was Rafe. These things haunted me. I was like a walking ghost searching for what I'd lost. I wasn't ready to let him go yet. Lucia needs time to sort this out on her own."

Noah lifted her hand to his lips. Her skin was paper thin and soft as tissue. She smiled at him tremulously when he leaned over and kissed her forehead.

"Thank you, Nonna. I'll try to be patient."

Her smile was slightly smug as she watched him stand. "I had a feeling that you were going to be the one. Ever since Rafe brought you home all skinny and haunted-looking, I knew."

He laughed then. "Well, you knew more than I did. Sometimes I still can't believe I'm this lucky."

Nonna regarded him for a long moment, her shrewd eyes moving over his face. It was tempting to squirm under the scrutiny but Noah forced himself to hold still. It mattered to him more than he'd ever thought it would to have her approval. She was the person that Rafe and Lucia had loved more than any other and he desperately wanted to know that she approved of him for her little girl.

"No, you wouldn't believe it, would you? Sweet boy. All you've ever known is disappointment and pain but this is for real. My *bambina* loves you. So this is not luck, this is fate. You are strong in all the ways she needs you to be. When she loses her way, you'll bring her back. Take care of her for me."

Noah hugged her gently. "Always."

Lucia moved her stapler to the left and organized the papers on the top of her desk into a neat pile. It should have been strange to be back at work after everything that had happened. Instead it was comforting. For once, all she had to do was focus on whatever ridiculous demands Adriana came up with and drink her coffee. Compared to worrying about killers and conspiracy theories, this was a breeze.

She took a long sip of her coffee and savored the witches' brew she couldn't live without. The coffee she made at home was never as good as what she got from a proper barista.

JJ had taken care of everything in her absence so she wasn't even coming back to a bunch of work. Honestly, it might have been better if she had been. That would have kept her mind too busy to focus on everything that had happened lately.

"So you went to the clock tower, and because you saw sunflower seeds, you think it means your brother is alive?" JJ said.

The way their cubicles were angled, she could only see a flash of her friend's blond hair every now and then while she moved around.

"Um, not exactly." Lucia wasn't sure how to respond. Especially since technically that was how it happened, but it sounded much crazier saying it aloud now that she wasn't in the moment.

Things were quiet for a moment before JJ leaned back again. "Sorry. I shouldn't have said it like that."

Lucia shrugged. "It's okay. We've always been honest with each other. Let's not change that now."

"True. But that doesn't mean I want to hurt you. You've been through so much lately. Hell, not just lately. Your mind is just trying to give you the one thing you want more than anything else. No wonder you saw sunflower seeds and came up with *my brother has risen from the dead*."

Lucia took another sip of her coffee. When put like that, she supposed it did sound a little crazy. All weekend she'd been over the evidence, if you could call it that, and had come up with a million and one scenarios that would explain how Rafe could be alive. She'd gone from the entire thing was an elaborate dream sequence to her brother was actually a mutant that was impervious to bullets.

But the one thing she wasn't willing to consider was that this was all a coincidence. Despite her conscious mind telling her it was ridiculous, there was a part of her that just couldn't let it go. Even if the other things could be explained, she hadn't imagined hearing Rafe's voice.

It might sound crazy to someone else, but she knew what she'd heard and it hadn't been grief or longing or whatever else Noah seemed to think she had going on. It had been in the heat of an extremely scary situation, the last place her mind would have been prone to delusions. After all, she'd adored Rafe, and her mind had no reason to associate him with some scary kidnapper.

But if it was Rafe, why would he have done that? He almost killed your friends.

Lucia brushed the thoughts away. She had no explanations for that part of things, but she'd figure it out.

"It's not just that. It's everything. The voice, the weird kidnapping attempts, and yes, the sunflower seeds. When you put it all together ..." Lucia held out her hands.

"Put it all together and you get a very thin case for something that is not likely to be true," JJ finished with a gentle smile. "This is all just speculation at this point. Let's not get ahead of ourselves."

Lucia reminded herself that her friend was just looking out for her and trying to keep her from getting hurt. JJ wasn't trying to hurt her feelings by dismissing the idea. Plus, she was objective enough to admit that if the tables were turned, she would be pretty sure that JJ was off her rocker to believe that someone dead and gone for six years was magically alive.

"I agree. It's early days, and there's no need for me to draw any concrete conclusions yet. All I'm doing is reporting to you what I experienced over the weekend. Also, Noah and I had insanely hot sex under that clock tower."

JJ leaned her head out of her cubicle so she could see Lucia. "You should have led with that. Damn girl, that's what I'm talking about! How is my favorite alpha asshole?"

"Cranky. And hot as hell. The usual."

Noah would probably object to the characterization, but it was definitely true. It made Lucia smile. He definitely was a cranky thing. Hot but cranky.

"God, you have all the luck. Ugh. Put in a good word for me with the sexy German, will you? That man looks like he was carved out of concrete." JJ made an exaggerated panting face and fanned herself dramatically.

Lucia laughed at the idea of putting in a good word with Oskar. He was so cantankerous that it was impossible to imagine him with the vivacious JJ. They'd probably kill each other inside of a week. Although knowing JJ, she'd kill him with sex. Oskar might not mind meeting his maker if that was how he got there.

"I'll tell him you said hello," she finally conceded.

JJ scoffed. "Don't tell him I said hello. Tell him I said I want to suck his—"

Adriana appeared at the edge of their cubicles, and JJ went silent. Lucia had just taken a large gulp of coffee and struggled to swallow it without sputtering or spitting it all over herself. Of course, a large portion of it went down the wrong way, and she ended up coughing like she was hacking up a lung. Adriana backed up a step with a look of disgust on her face.

Lucia sucked in a few breaths and then cleared her throat. "Sorry."

Adriana ignored her and instead turned around to speak to someone behind her. "And this is where the real work is done, Mr. Nelson. I pride myself on having the best and brightest in the fashion industry. It takes a great team to create the fashions you saw on the runway."

Lucia refrained from rolling her eyes. Every so often Adriana would bring investors around to see how they operated and to convince them to part with their money to fund her international expansion. That was the only time she seemed to think that what they did was a 'team effort.' On any other occasion, it was all Adriana, all the time.

"Jessica Jones is our extremely talented makeup

artist who has been instrumental in creating our signature runway looks. And this is Lucia DeMarco, a design intern who shows great promise."

Adriana widened her eyes at them as if to say, *look alive*, so JJ stood and extended her hand.

"Nice to meet you, Mr. Nelson. I hope you'll be joining the Adriana Fashions family soon."

JJ was smiling so widely that Lucia could tell the guy had to be cute. She only acted like this around the investors she thought were hot. Lucia pasted a smile on her face but couldn't see past JJ since her friend was still hanging on to his hand. She was glad that JJ was so good at the schmoozing stuff because she wasn't. All she'd ever wanted was to hole up and work on her own designs, not convince someone else that it was worthwhile.

"Glad to meet the people on the front lines. Perhaps I could get a tour while I'm here. Miss DeMarco could show me around, perhaps?"

At the sound of her name, Lucia choked slightly on the last sip of coffee. Adriana frowned at her, and she hurriedly grabbed the napkin from her lap to dab at her lips.

"Sure, I mean … of course. I can give you a tour. There's not much to see though."

"There's plenty to see," Adriana interjected with a sideways look at Lucia that was sharp enough to cut glass. "Show him the samples closet and the design floor at least."

"Yes ma'am. Follow me, Mr. Nelson."

He stepped from behind Adriana, and Lucia immediately noticed the cut of his suit. It fit perfectly and looked like it had been designed and tailored just for him. Then he turned his head and she got her first look at his face and realized why his voice had sounded so familiar.

The coffee cup in her hand fell and would have hit the floor, but his hand shot out and caught it in midair. He placed it gently on the edge of her desk.

"Careful. We don't want to make a mess, do we?" His eyes narrowed meaningfully as Lucia just stared with her mouth open.

It was Rafe.

Chapter Six

Lucia's heart thundered against her ribs. She tried to drag in a deep breath, but her breathing was shallow and thin. She wanted to turn around and ask JJ why she hadn't recognized him. He was wearing what was obviously a wig, since it was threaded liberally with gray hair, and a thin pair of wire-framed glasses obscured his eyes. But it was him. It was Rafe. She'd been right.

You're not crazy. He's here.

For the life of her, she couldn't think of one word to say to her brother. After six long years where she'd grieved him, and missed him, and was so desperate to talk to him sometimes she talked to herself, she couldn't think of a single thing to say.

"Miss DeMarco, right after you."

She could only stare at him. He was waiting for her. Her boss was waiting for her. Everyone was waiting for her to do something, say something. Somewhere Ryan was in the building. All she had to do was push her panic button and he'd come running, and the whole team would have her immediate GPS location.

Ryan was there to protect her ... from Rafe ... *her brother*. She spent several long seconds debating what to do, what to say, and how to say it. But in the end, she just pushed her hair back and forced a smile.

Unashamed

"Of course. Follow me."

At her side, Rafe smiled and nodded at her coworkers, while Lucia tried to get her nerves under control. Her hands were sweaty, so she wiped them on her slacks. Once they left the main pen and emerged into the hallway, Lucia turned to face him. It was a shock all over again, to see him here out in the open like this. She repressed the urge to reach over and pinch him to see if he was real.

"Why are you doing this?"

Despite the wig and the glasses, the smile Rafe turned on her was pleasant and familiar. It reminded her of summers at Coney Island, teasing pillow fights, and brotherly hugs. It reminded her of a lifetime ago when his smiling at her like this would have been no big deal.

It reminded her of a lifetime she'd been robbed of.

Rafe's pleasant smile fell like he could sense her thoughts. "There's plenty of time for asking questions. Just give me a moment."

The shudders racked her body. She tried to keep her hands still by clasping them together in front of her tightly. Where was Ryan? Was he going to find them? Was he going to hurt Rafe? Was Rafe going to hurt him? The fear of either of those things happening was the only thing that kept her from pushing her panic button.

Rafe had already hurt Ryan once before, when he'd broken into her apartment. She'd never forget the sight of Ryan slumped over in that chair, looking like a broken doll. The only member of Blake Security that Rafe hadn't yet hurt was Dylan. She didn't want to give him that opportunity. It made her sad to have the thought, but she couldn't trust her brother. An entire lifetime had passed between now and when they'd eaten funnel cake together. This man was capable of anything and she could never forget that.

"I don't even know you anymore," she whispered.

He stiffened next to her, but his expression never altered. "Lulu, I know you're concerned." Anyone watching would think they were having a friendly conversation about maybe the weather, or how she really must try some divine Italian restaurant next time she was in Italy. It was a charming smile. It was also the smile of a killer.

He's still your brother.

"Follow me," he said to her with that false smile. She would never understand how he got the smile to reach his eyes as if he meant every word. And then it hit her. Men like Rafe, men like Noah, men like Matthias—this was what they were trained to do.

Lie, kill, betray.

He directed her, even though it appeared to everyone who passed as if she was giving him the grand tour. He led her down the back stairwell. Down to the next floor where hair and makeup was, and then down to garment repair.

As soon as they hit the third floor, he visibly relaxed. "Okay, through here there's a laundry chute. It'll put you into one of the laundry baskets. Not to worry; that's the one I've got marked to go to my van. I need to walk upstairs and do the whole routine before your security figures out you're missing. We leave in exactly seven minutes. Do you understand?"

He turned her toward the door, but she couldn't move. All she could do was stare at him, bile rising in her throat. Her heart hammered behind her ribcage, and her lungs refused to cooperate. This was her brother. *She needed to do something*. But she couldn't move. It was like her legs had gone wooden or become encased in lead.

"Rafe, what is going on?"

"Lulu, I will explain everything as soon as I have you to safety." He took her arm gently and pushed her toward the hallway where the laundry facilities were.

She tugged her arm free of his hold. "You've been trying to hurt me."

His dark gaze focused on her. "Listen to what you just said. My whole life, my one and only goal has been to protect you. Do you think that I would ever hurt you?"

"But you tried to take me. You broke into my place. You tried to hurt me." Her legs wobbled and she stumbled backward.

He held his hands up. "I didn't try to hurt you. Think it through, Lulu. I broke into your apartment the first time to try and get you away from Noah's men. I tried to grab you at your fashion show. I underestimated that they'd have an ORUS operative watching you. And I tried to take you again from the penthouse. Take you. *Not hurt you*."

"You hurt my friends."

"Those men are not your friends. Those men are killers. Every last one of them. I trained Noah myself so I know what he's capable of. He's not your friend."

"And I should trust you?" She laughed bitterly at the thought that he was judging Noah when he'd done something so much worse. He'd lied to her and let her mourn for years. For nothing!

"Yes. I'm your brother."

She tipped her chin up to meet his gaze. "Oh yeah, then where have you been for six years? When I was grieving, when Nonna was grieving, where were you? I buried you. The only person I had to lean on was Noah. *Where were you?*"

He opened his mouth, and then it snapped shut. "Lucia, I'm not going to get another chance like this. Come with me. I'll explain everything. You'll understand."

She wanted to. She wanted to trust him. She wanted to believe in him. But it hurt. The six years of compounded pain and loss, they hurt. Not to mention, she didn't think his plan was going to work. If she didn't show up on the cameras any second, Ryan would be on to them. Then Dylan, Matthias, Noah, Jonas, Oskar, all the people she cared about, they would engage with her brother. And somebody she cared about was going to get hurt again.

She pulled back. "I can't. We can't just leave."

"Yes, you can. It's easy. Walk through that door." He gestured toward the laundry room holding aside the plastic door dividers. "You get in the laundry chute, you land in my basket, you get moved onto my truck, and I take you to safety. That's the plan. Simple. You think I exposed myself because I want to hurt you?"

"I don't know why you're here. I wished and prayed you would be alive. And now you're here. But I love Noah. I can't just leave."

He jerked as if he'd been slapped. "I knew he was watching you. But I didn't think you'd fallen in love with him. You're too young to know what he's capable of."

"I know what he's capable of. I know what *you're* capable of. He told me all about it. You trained him to be a killer."

Rafe winced. "I know. There's a lot to explain. But you can't trust him. He's the reason I've been gone for six years."

She shook her head. "I remember that day. I remember he shot you. Clearly you're still alive. But I remember how it happened. You stepped in front of a target. It wasn't like Noah sought you out and hurt you. You did that."

His dark eyes searched her face. "Lucia, there's so much you don't understand."

"I'm not leaving until I do."

His watch beeped. "Shit. We're out of time. Go. Please, I'm begging you."

She shook her head. "No. It's time for me to go. If I'm not up there in a second, Ryan is going to come looking for me. And I don't want either one of you hurt."

He ran his hand through his hair roughly. "Are you kidding me? You're seriously in love with the enemy?"

"I'm in love with *Noah*. He's a good man. And I can't just walk away."

He checked his watch again. "Out of time. Let's go back."

He took her by the elbow and his touch was gentle, but still dominant. He knew exactly where he needed her to go. Exactly which path would avoid any cameras. And then they were on the main floor again and he eased his hold on her, put on that smile again, as if they'd had the most pleasant stroll in the world.

"Well, thank you very much for a lovely tour, Miss DeMarco." And then he leaned closer to her and whispered, "I'll find you again."

And then her brother was gone.

"Boss, we've got a problem."

Noah looked up from his computer and rubbed his bleary eyes. Being tired wasn't anything new but the events of the past couple of weeks had taken him to a new level of exhaustion. Not to mention it was an adjustment being in a new place. They'd had all their stuff packed and brought over, but nothing was in the right places and he'd spent a ludicrous amount of time just searching for his mouse the first day he'd tried to use the computer. But in the end, they'd gotten their shit together. Their offices may have been shot up to hell but Blake Security still had work to do. They had open cases and clients who were depending on them.

"What's up, Matthias?"

He put his computer to sleep so he could give the kid his full attention. Matthias had gone back to work a few days after the attack, over Noah's objections. He seemed fine, but there was something so cold and reserved about him. Noah had tried a couple of times to get him to talk about that night in the penthouse but he'd said he was fine. Whatever the hell that meant. If he didn't seem to settle in soon, Noah was going to pull him out of the field permanently. They were short staffed, but having a loose cannon in the field was potentially more dangerous.

"We've got a problem. One of the guests who logged

in for Adriana Fashions today was using an alias. There were layers upon layers of background laid so on first glance, everything was fine. But like always, I kept the decryption algorithm running. Just in case. Around lunchtime, it started to pull back the layers. There were five or six. Which is why it took so long to see it, but Andrew Nelson doesn't exist. He's not real."

Noah's heart stopped. "Fuck. *Fuck*."

He pushed himself to standing then dragged his phone out of his pocket. The only thing swirling around his brain was Lucia.

Lucia, Lucia, Lucia.

"Pull the camera footage from the office. All of the goddamn cameras."

"Already done. They've been running on a continuous loop all damn day, since about 9:15 this morning. The bitch of it is I can't even see when they would've inserted that loop. The guy is good. Whoever it is, whoever did this—"

Noah tried to remember his training. Tried to stay calm and in control. He took a deep breath before he responded. It wasn't the kid's fault that he was about to lose his mind. "Find me some goddamned cameras that can see who went in and out of that building. Pull every camera from the surrounding buildings."

"Already on it. I'll let you know as soon as I have something."

That made Noah feel a little better. He should have known that Matthias would be all over this. He took any breach of security personally. Quickly, Noah called Ryan's number. And waited not-so-patiently as three rings went by.

When Ryan finally answered, he sounded out of breath. "What's up, Boss?"

"Where the fuck is Lucia?"

There was a pause before Ryan said, "She's right here. You want to talk to her?"

The bottom dropped out of his stomach. She was safe? She was okay? Noah's hands shook. He forced himself to drag in a deep breath. "Yes. Please put her on."

"Noah?" Her voice was soft. "What's the matter?"

Shit. Her voice was a soothing balm over the raw frayed ends of his nerves. "Oh, baby, I just needed to hear your voice. Did you have a good day?"

She hesitated for a moment. Noah's internal radar went crazy in those few moments. What was she hiding? Was there someone there with her forcing her to respond a certain way? Well, no. He'd just spoken to Ryan. But could

Unashamed

Ryan really be trusted? In the span of five seconds, his mind spun through a loop of worst-case scenarios until Lucia finally sighed.

"Yes. An average day. Are you sure everything's okay?"

Things had been tense between them since she'd made her confession the other day. She'd told him what she thought was going on and he'd reacted badly. She knew he didn't believe her. Noah cursed himself. He should have been more supportive and then worked her around to the idea of seeing a professional. Instead he'd been harsh with her and hadn't taken the time to reassure her. The trust they'd worked so hard to earn, the groundwork for their relationship, was rotting at the edges and he wasn't sure what to do about it.

But he knew the truth. Rafe was gone. The longer she clung on to that delusion, the more worried he became. But for right now, he'd settle for her safety.

"Yep. I can't just call to hear my girl's voice?"

"Okay, if you say so. But why didn't you just call me?"

He sighed. She had him there. And then he went back to what he did best. He lied. "I was calling Ryan for a status update, anyway. Figured I'd kill two birds with one stone."

Lucia giggled. "Well, that's going to make the phone sex a lot more awkward. But if Ryan's cool with it, then—"

All Noah heard next was Ryan's voice. "Sorry, Boss. Not with my phone. You can call her later. I'm not letting you torture me by making me listen to that. It's already bad enough that I walked in on you guys in the gym."

Noah winced. Yeah, he was going to have to work at a more private arrangement for all of them. This place might be more secure, but it was smaller than the penthouse. And sooner or later, it wasn't going to work anymore. Noah needed to figure out if they were ever going to go back to the penthouse. He had a *lot* of things to figure out.

He ran a legitimate business, and that business needed a base of operations. Right now this would do, but it wasn't a long-term solution. Nor was it a good home base for him and Lucia. Sooner or later they'd have to look at a good permanent option. *Permanent.* For once the word didn't scare him. Now when he closed his eyes and imagined the future, he could see it clearly. Him and Lucia together, with however many kids she wanted. He would do whatever he had to for Lucia to have everything she deserved.

But for now, their downtown hideout would have to do. He would make it work until he was sure she was safe.

"Ryan, keep this quiet, but it seems one of the visitors to Lucia's building today was using an alias. Were there any anomalies that you were aware of?"

Ryan replied slowly. "No. I would have called it in. Everything looked good. Should I go route number two?"

After what had happened at the penthouse, they'd taken the time to map out various alternate routes from Lucia's job back to their new home base, trying to take into account various scenarios and the possibility of traffic.

"Yes. And Ryan?"

"Yeah Boss?"

"Please bring her home safe."

Chapter Seven

Unashamed

As soon as Lucia walked in, Noah wrapped her in his arms and lifted her off the ground. She squealed at the sudden motion but her alarm quickly morphed into heat when his head nestled into the crook of her neck. She wasn't even sure what he was doing, breathing her in? Whatever he was doing, it felt amazing. She tipped her head to the side to allow him better access to the soft skin of her neck which ignited under his caress.

A throat cleared behind them, and Lucia was reminded of where they were, in the entryway where anyone could see them. She turned slightly and caught Ryan's amused smile as he walked past them to the kitchen. Lucia blushed. She hadn't even taken her coat off. Embarrassment warred with desire as she glanced back at Noah. The man could make her forget her own name sometimes!

She pulled back and adjusted her clothing. "Wow, this is quite a welcome. What's going on with you today?"

He held her tighter, resting his head on top of hers. It was so uncharacteristically tender that for a moment, she wondered if he knew. Could he sense her duplicity? Did betrayal have a scent?

Stop it, she chided herself. She wasn't betraying Noah by not telling him about Rafe's visit. The situation was complicated and she was only trying to make sure that no one got hurt. There was a long, tense history between the two men and it wouldn't take much to set it off like a powder keg. If she wanted them all to be standing at the end, it was crucial that she handle things properly.

First things first, figuring out just what the hell her brother was up to and where he'd been all these years. It wouldn't be easy to keep a level head in this situation. She'd wanted Rafe back for so long but she couldn't ignore the many ways his death had changed her. She was no longer the innocent, naïve girl who accepted things at face value. Grief and loss had taught her what a bitch life could be, and she wasn't ready to just accept Rafe back into her life without understanding his motives. Because now that she was older and wiser, she understood that everyone had an agenda, even her beloved brother. He'd come back for a reason. Why now? And why did she have the horrible feeling that his agenda was to hurt Noah and the rest of her new family?

"Nothing has gotten into me. Just missing my girl." Noah kissed her forehead before setting her on her feet.

The sound of Ryan's gagging behind them made Lucia giggle. Noah just raised both middle fingers before grabbing her arm and leading her down the hallway to their room. As they passed Matthias's room, Lucia paused.

"Is he sleeping?"

Noah nodded. "He's doing better. He's been working every day but gets tired earlier than usual. Hell, I probably should have insisted he take more time but we need him too much."

Lucia placed a hand on the doorjamb, torn between wanting to go in and see her friend and fear that he wouldn't want her there. Not that she didn't deserve his derision, but if she saw that look on Matthias's face it would kill her.

It brought home everything she'd learned today in a whole new way. These men had put their lives on the line for her not knowing the whole truth. Would they still stand for her if they found out that it was her brother who was targeting them? The whole situation was her fault. Matthias wouldn't have been beaten up if her insane brother wasn't playing some sort of game. Whether she'd meant to or not, her curiosity, or stubbornness--whatever you wanted to call it--had brought this whole thing down on them.

"He's going to be fine."

She turned to see Noah's knowing look. As usual he could read her mind. Though she was glad for once that he couldn't *actually* read her mind, otherwise he'd know how much she was hiding from him.

"I know. Still doesn't make it easy to see him like that. Especially since it's because of me."

Noah pulled her gently, steering her toward their room. Once they were inside, he shut the door behind him gently then flicked the lock with a twist of his wrist. Her pulse instantly sped up. She couldn't even play it cool, not when her panties got instantly damp at the knowledge that she and Noah were now alone.

"Oh, now I see why you missed me."

His lips turned up but he didn't bother to respond. Just spread his fingers through her hair and yanked her toward him until their mouths clashed in a furious erotic clinch.

It was a shock to be treated so roughly, especially coming from Noah. Everyone saw him as such a badass but he'd only ever touched her with tenderness. He held her like spun glass or like a mirage that he was afraid would disappear at any moment.

Like she was a goddess and he was unworthy.

When in truth, she was the one who felt unworthy. Noah had many hidden layers but they were all out of necessity. Everything he'd ever done had been to protect her. Lucia tightened her arms around his neck and savored the slide of his tongue against hers. Would he still want her if he knew that she wasn't as noble? The things she was concealing, was it for his benefit or her own?

Just who was she protecting?

"I've been waiting all day for this. Thinking about what I'd do. How I'd do it." He spoke in jerky tones as he stripped her clothes from her body.

Lucia moaned when his teeth sank into her shoulder. She hadn't even known that she could make these sounds, wild, wanton and completely untamed. Emotions roiled inside and amplified the desire until it was all she could feel. Guilt, lust and shame were a heady combination.

"Show me," she panted. Their eyes met and something dark and dangerous sparked in his eyes. "Show me everything you imagined."

It was obvious when his control finally snapped. Noah growled and hitched her legs around his waist. They'd barely made it onto the bed, pressing and humping against each other while standing before they fell in a heap onto the comforter, desperately undressing each other. Lucia gripped the linen between her fingers as his head dipped and followed the curve of her spine. When his mouth settled between her thighs, she reared up with a hoarse shout.

"Yes. Give it all to me." He pressed her back down with a firm hand on her stomach and the sensation of being restrained sent her straight over the edge.

She came hard as he teased her clit with his tongue, staying with her as she squirmed helplessly against wave after wave of pleasure. When it ended, she was exhausted and wrung out. Then he sat up and slid in with one thrust, bringing her right to the edge again.

"*Fuck*. Nothing in the world will ever be better than this."

Lucia grabbed at his hair, needing something to anchor her as he rode her hard. He was completely absorbed in her, rubbing his nose against her neck like he just needed to be connected to her from head to toe. She felt the same way, like she would take him into her soul if she could. Nothing should ever come between them and the knowledge that her lies could do just that scared her to death.

"I love you, Noah. No matter what happens." She needed him to know how she felt. Because there was a part of her that was terrified he'd never understand what she'd done.

His head fell back while his face twisted with pleasure. She could tell he was getting close by the low, sexy sounds he was making and the bunch and tense of his muscles beneath her hands.

"Nothing is going to happen. Except you are going to come for me again. *Now*."

She couldn't deny him anything when he rasped it in that demanding voice. Desire curled through her veins, started low in the pit of her belly and radiating outward until she was crying out with every thrust. Noah tensed and then whispered her name, and that was what sent her over. She clung to him weakly as every one of her muscles seized, clenching around him like they never wanted to let go. Like they were afraid to let go.

As he finally fell to the side next to her, exhausted, Lucia could only hope that she would never have to. Or that he'd forgive her if she did.

As Noah rested, completely exhausted and sated, he should have been thinking of nothing except how amazing that had been. Instead all he could concentrate on was the nagging sense that Lucia was hiding something from him.

For one, she hadn't looked him in the eye except for when she was reassuring him that she loved him no matter what. Why did she suddenly feel the need to make that distinction?

He pulled her closer, nestling against her back and absorbing the comforting heat of her body. She was always so cuddly after sex and although Noah wouldn't have thought it possible, so was he. He loved sharing body heat with her and wrapping her in his arms. It was the time when he felt closest to her and after the day he'd had, he needed it.

Lucia apparently wasn't in the same place. After wiggling around to get free, she sat up and stretched, the sheet sliding down to reveal the tips of berry nipples. "I have so much work to catch up on."

Noah's body responded with a predictable clinch. Damn she was perfect. Lucia either didn't notice or care that her nipples had burst free because she was squirming and stretching without a care to the way she was arousing him. His eyes must have given him away because she gathered the sheets to her chest, hiding her breasts from his view. Her cheeks flushed, but he could tell she was pleased by the way her eyes crinkled at the corners. She'd come a long way in recent weeks, going from a shy, hesitant lover to slowly coming into confidence in her sexuality. It was an honor to be witness to her blossoming. It also made him want to drag her back under the covers and not let her up anytime soon. Since he knew she wouldn't go for that, he tried desperately to think of something to distract him from the enticing bounce of her full breasts as she moved.

"Sorry things are a bit cramped here. I know it's hard to find room to think when there are so many people on top of each other."

She tilted her head adorably. "You're apologizing for keeping us all safe?"

Relief that she got it spread through him. "When you put it like that, no, I'm not."

"Good. Because you're doing the best you can, Noah. That's all anyone can do. And for the record, your best is pretty damn good."

She leaned over and kissed him gently. The sweetness of the kiss caught him off guard, sending a bolt of pure longing and awe through him. Would he ever get used to the idea that she was actually his? He watched her dress, his heart flipping over as she kept glancing at him with intimate little looks that made him feel like he was ten feet tall.

He hoped he never got used to her, to them together. Noah never wanted to forget how fortunate he was to have someone to love and who loved him in return.

"Let me know when you're ready for dinner. I promised Jonas that we'd get burgers tonight. I think he's going through withdrawals."

"Oh, thank you! I thought I was the only one. Home-cooked meals are awesome but if I don't get something greasy and fattening in my system soon I'm going to lose it."

Noah chuckled. As long as they'd been together, Lucia had been harassing him to eat better and just take better care of himself in general. So he couldn't resist the opportunity to tease her for missing junk food.

"You know, I've been trying to eat better like you said."

Lucia gave him a death glare. "Don't even start. I have been through too much in the past couple of weeks to care about the state of my arteries. I want grease and fat, and I want it *now*."

"Yes, ma'am. Your wish is my command."

Lucia leaned over the bed and kissed him, her lips lingering against his until Noah was hard as a rock. He reached under the sheet and grasped his cock firmly, squeezing just below the head until he didn't feel as though he was in danger of coming just from the sound of her voice.

"Say that again," she whispered.

"Anything you want is yours, baby. You know that."

"Good because what I want is the most fattening, delicious burger in the state of New York."

Lucia winked at him before leaving the room, pulling the door closed behind her.

Noah was in the middle of dressing when someone knocked on the door. He pulled his shirt over his head hastily before stalking over to the door and yanking it open. Then he blinked when he saw that it was Matthias standing there.

"Can I come in? I have something to show you."

Noah stepped back and allowed him to enter the room. Although Matthias had been insisting for days that he was fine, he was still slightly pale. The bruises had faded but there were dark shadows under his eyes, making him look gaunt.

"I was finally able to pull camera footage from the bank across the street. Their encryption was pretty decent so it took a little longer than I expected. You have to see this to believe it."

He held out his tablet, and Noah turned it around to see the image displayed. It took him a moment to process what he was seeing, but when it finally sank in, his breath left his lungs in a sudden sharp exhalation. The edges of his vision went gray, and he would have fallen if Matthias hadn't clapped him on the shoulder.

"You okay, Boss?" Matthias peered at him with concern.

Noah pounded on his own chest, trying to jumpstart his heart. "Rafe. This is Rafe," he repeated needlessly.

Matthias brought the tablet closer and stared at the image as if that would somehow make it clearer. The man pictured was in profile, but Noah would never forget that face. He'd stood by his side and watched that profile for years, after all.

Matthias touched the screen, and it switched to another image. In this one, Rafe faced the camera and the shock of seeing him hit Noah all over again. He was wearing glasses, no doubt to hide his face since Rafe had always had perfect vision, and a suit that looked expensive. His friend was definitely older, his dark hair threaded through with gray at the temples and above the ears, but it was undeniably Rafe.

"This is not possible." He stared. How was this possible? How was she right?

Matthias frowned and then glanced down at the image. "Wait, when you say that's Rafe, you don't mean–"

"That's Rafael DeMarco. Lucia's brother."

Matthias stared at him blankly. "I thought her brother was dead?"

"I thought he was, too. Especially since I'm the one who killed him." Six long years ago. The grief and the shame had almost killed him.

Noah turned the tablet off, unable to stomach looking at his old friend's treacherous face any longer. A million thoughts clamored for space in his brain but at the forefront was, *What the hell am I supposed to tell Lucia?* Except … she'd tried to tell him, hadn't she? He'd assumed she was losing it. That the pressure had been too much. But she'd been right.

And you didn't believe her.

"What are we going to do?" Matthias finally asked. His face was a blank mask, but that didn't fool Noah. The kid would have questions, along with all of the others.

The things he'd done in his past were coming back to haunt them all, and it was only fair for them to expect answers since they were the ones paying the price. Matthias had taken a brutal beating and Jonas could have lost his sight, so if their injuries had anything to do with his skeletons falling out of the closet, they had the right to some answers.

But first, he had to ask the right questions. Because with how strange Lucia had been acting all day he couldn't ignore the very real possibility that she had more than an inkling that Rafe was alive. Something that went beyond hearing his voice that night. Something more concrete, like seeing him.

"Nothing. You are not going to do anything. He was in the building with Lucia, but he obviously didn't hurt her. So that's not his end game."

The kid frowned. "Do you really think he'd hurt his own sister?"

"Hell if I know. He's not the same guy I once knew, obviously. I can't pretend to understand what he would or wouldn't do. So I'm going to ask the only person who might know."

"Lucia. Shit, this is going to get ugly." Matthias shook his head. "You really think she knows?"

"God, I hope not." Noah took the tablet and tucked it under his arm. "She and I are going to have a little talk."

Unashamed

Chapter Eight

Unashamed

Noah wasn't sure whether to be furious with Lucia, or thrilled that she was right. Either way, they needed to have it out. She'd made love to him not two hours ago, but when she'd looked at him and told him she loved him, she'd been lying to him.

She didn't lie; she kept it to herself. Damn it. Keeping a secret like this was tantamount to lying. How the hell was he supposed to keep her safe, keep them *all* safe if she didn't tell him the most pertinent information of all? As much as he wanted to justify it, he couldn't deny the bitter tang of betrayal on his tongue.

He found her in the living room, cross-legged on the couch, wearing one of his shirts and a pair of his boxer shorts. She had the sleeves rolled up to reveal her slim forearms. Head bent over, she was going through a stack of fashion magazines labeling things and putting Post-its on them. Writing things like, *Pull*, *Check with Adriana if we have it*, and *Can we partner with this designer?*

She was working. Completely in her zone. Well, too bad for her; Noah was about to interrupt her. He marched over to the couch, and she looked up, giving him the sweetest smile he'd ever seen. So sweet it pulled at the places in his heart he'd have sworn didn't exist anymore. She looked so perfect there, the lamp on the table creating soft shadows and halos all over her. She looked like an angel.

"Hi. What's up?" There was an invitation in her smile and, like the traitor it was, his dick swelled. He couldn't seem to keep his mind or his hands off of her. But they needed to talk, so the big guy downstairs would just have to wait.

"I was going to ask you the same thing. Is there anything you want to talk to me about?"

Her brows furrowed even as she continued smiling up at him. "No. I mean, unless when you say *talk*, you mean—" She lifted a brow and her eyes danced mischievously.

Okay, so he could totally understand how even the most hardened spies could fall for the enemy. Because right about now, he wasn't using the brain cells God gave him. He was using the other part of his brain. The one completely responsible for manning the sex train. The one that wanted to yank off her boxers and sink into her, right here in the middle of the living room, where anyone could walk in.

No. Stay strong. Besides, they'd done enough of that. After one too many close calls, the tracking devices he had everyone wear were now used to track where he and Lucia were, so the team could give them a wide berth.

Unashamed

Not exactly the use he had planned for them, but whatever. They had enough privacy. And maybe if he just sank deep into her, he'd stop riding the razor's edge and focus enough so he could ask her what he needed to ask her. If he slid the boxers off, spread her wide and stroked deep, they'd both feel better. They'd be relaxed enough to have this conversation. It was amazing the things he could come up with when he let his dick do the thinking.

He considered it. For a long moment, he considered it. She'd taste so sweet. Was she sore from earlier? Or, from this morning? He hadn't exactly been gentle. But then again, neither had she. He still had her nail marks on his shoulders. Noah grinned with purely male satisfaction. He could still feel how those scratches had stung this morning in the shower when the water hit them.

Oh shit. He did not need to think about the shower, or what they did in there.

And he probably shouldn't think about her taste because then he'd think about what they'd just done and— no. Never mind, there it was. In amazing Technicolor and surround sound in his mind. He cleared his throat.

No. They were having this conversation now. Because he was pretty damn certain that after they had this conversation, the last thing on his mind would be sex.

"Nope. Nothing to talk about."

Her gaze searched his. And he saw pain there. He hated that he'd had a part in the pain there. Because he was pretty damn sure there was one thing she probably wanted to talk about, but she didn't trust him to be open-minded. That hurt more than anything else, that she couldn't talk to him. Didn't she understand that all he wanted was her safety and happiness?

Behind his back, Noah's fingers tightened around the tablet he held. A tablet that held the image of a ghost he'd long since buried. A ghost that was back to haunt them all. The question was what did he want?

Noah took the tablet with the photo on display from behind his back and slapped it on the table. "Explain."

Lucia glanced at the picture, and her breath caught. Her fingers flew to her lips then her gaze flickered to his. "I don't know what to say."

"Matthias came into my office freaking the fuck out because Nelson came back as a false name. I lost years off of my life in that split second when I was worried about you."

"Noah, I can explain."

He shook his head. "I was terrified that something happened to you. Terrified that once again I was too late. And then I called Ryan and everything was fine. So I need to know what's going on. After everything we've been through, I would have thought honesty was a given. Then Matthias showed me something that should be impossible. Something you already knew."

"I didn't lie to you, Noah."

He crossed his arms. "Oh yeah? Then what do you call it exactly? Omission? You just happened to forget that you saw your brother in your office today?" He kneeled down so their gazes were level. "Or please, tell me you didn't see him. Please fucking tell me he came into your office but you didn't see him. Tell me that so that I don't think the woman I love lied to me."

She pushed herself off the couch and shoved at his chest. Not that she could move him, but still. Noah didn't know what he'd expected. How he'd expected her to respond. All he knew was he hadn't expected this. He'd never seen her like this before.

"How dare you? How dare you stand there and call me a liar because I didn't tell you I saw him. That I didn't tell you that he showed up at my office, unannounced, as some kind of potential investor. Don't stand there acting like I knew what was going to happen and deliberately deceived you. No, I didn't tell you I saw him. No, I didn't tell you he asked me to leave with him. But why would I?

You would have had me fitted for a lovely white jacket with funky straps. *Fuck you*, Noah. I tried to tell you I saw Rafe already, remember? I wasn't too eager for you to tell me I'm crazy again."

That did make him stagger. He didn't think he'd ever heard her use the word *fuck* before. He'd never seen her this furious. After everything they'd been through over the years, she'd never gone off on him like this before.

"Lucia, I didn't say you're crazy."

"Oh didn't you? You insinuated it. Tried to make me think that my mind was playing tricks on me. That I wanted to think he was back, so I fabricated it all. The damn sunflower seeds, the voice when he tried to take me from the penthouse. I thought I was losing it. I needed you to be in my corner. I needed you to tell me we'd figure it out. Hell, even if you'd said, 'I think someone's deliberately fucking with you,' that would've been far better than, 'Lucia, princess, your mind is playing tricks on you.' You might as well have taken out a billboard saying 'This bitch is crazy.'"

They squared off against each other as he stared down at her. "I never called you crazy."

"Bullshit. Did you or did you not think I needed a shrink?"

Unashamed

He opened his mouth then snapped it shut. *Fuck*.
"Look, I was worried. I love you and I was watching you drown."

"Well, how was I supposed to feel when I thought my brother was back? And newsflash, turns out he is. Turns out I wasn't crazy and losing my shit after all."

"Lu —"

"Don't you dare start with me. I told you. You didn't believe me. That hurt. It hurt so deep."

She started to shake then wrapped her arms around herself and rocked back on her heels. All he wanted to do was hold her. He hated this, what they were doing to each other. Hated that he'd fucked up.

She was right. She'd tried to tell him. But he'd only seen it one way and if he was going to figure out what his old friend was up to, he needed to be able to look at it from all angles. He didn't want this to be their undoing, so he gritted his teeth, knowing she was going to fight him, but he wrapped his arms around her anyway, rocking their bodies together.

"I'm sorry. I'm so fucking sorry. I saw the picture and I lost it. I almost lost you that night. I almost lost three of my friends. I just couldn't see what you were seeing. And that's no excuse because I should've believed you. I love you. You are my entire world and I should've trusted in you."

Against his chest she sobbed wildly. He kept hold of her until eventually she wrapped her arms around him and he breathed a sigh of relief. They might not be okay right now, but they would be. Because she loved him too. And she wasn't going to stop no matter how dicey things got.

"Let's try this again. Tell me what happened today."

Against his chest, she whispered everything that happened in her office. Rafe trying to direct her out and away. And how he'd told her not to trust Noah or anyone that worked for him.

Noah frowned in confusion. If he was alive and keeping tabs on his sister, Rafe had to know that Noah had left ORUS by now. Was something else going on? All he knew was his best friend was back from the dead. And had tried to kill him and/or his men on more than one occasion. So right now, Noah didn't fucking trust Rafe at all. Certainly not with Lucia's life.

Noah wasn't sure how long he held her, but eventually she started to relax into his arms, and he picked her up, carrying her to the couch before setting her on his lap. "Please forgive me. I was worried. But I should've listened."

She nodded. "I'm sorry. I should've told you. I wanted to; I just wasn't sure how you'd react."

He licked his lips. "Can I ask you a question?"

She nodded.

"Why didn't you go with him? Having him back is all you've ever wanted."

Lucia eyes settled on his and what he saw there rocked him. Complete love and trust.

"I love you. I couldn't just leave you like that. I knew how much you'd worry and honestly, I'm not sure how much I should trust him. He let me and Nonna grieve for him. He put us through torture. And you too. He's hurt Ryan, Matthias, Jonas, and Oskar. I love Rafe. And part of me is so full with joy that he's alive, but I don't know what's going on. But one thing I know for sure is that you love me and would never let anyone hurt me. So I stayed."

His gaze searched hers. "I would absolutely come for you. I would turn over every corner of this earth to find you if he'd taken you away from me."

She nodded. "That's part of what I'm afraid of. Starting some war with you and Rafe. We're already in the middle of a war. One I don't understand and I don't know how to stop. I didn't want anyone else getting hurt on my behalf. Not you, not him. Or anyone here. All of you are my family so I just didn't say anything. Sorry if I compromised anyone's safety."

He nodded. "I get it. I shouldn't have asked you to choose."

"So what do we do now?"

"If I know your brother, he'll try again. But he's certainly not going to talk to me. He's not going to come to us head on. ORUS trained him too well. He wants you."

"So what are we supposed to do?"

"I think I need you to wear a wire."

She stared at him. "Are you kidding me right now? You want me to wear a wire the next time I talk to my brother? Whenever that is."

Noah sighed. "This is Rafe. He won't wait long before he contacts you again. If you have any other suggestions for the best way to get him to talk to me, I'm open. I'd love to get to the business of finding out who's trying to hurt you. I'm all ears. For the time being, we need to find out what's going on with him. Where has he been? And given that he tried to kill several members of my team, I don't think he'll be willing to talk. But if anyone can get through to him, it would be you. We need to call a cease-fire for now and look at the bigger picture. Do you have a better idea?"

She chewed her bottom lip. "I don't, but it doesn't mean I have to like this one."

Chapter Nine

If Lucia thought Noah was relentless when he

wanted something, she hadn't seen anything. She'd seriously underestimated her best friend. She'd been dodging JJ's calls ever since leaving work early on Friday. Normally they would have hung out or at least spoken every day but Lucia had no idea what to say to her friend. How could she even begin to explain the shit show of her life? Even thinking about explaining everything that had happened lately made her tired. Truthfully, all she wanted to do was stay in bed and pull the covers over her head.

She thought her method of dealing was working pretty well until Noah appeared at the door of their room one night holding out his phone and wearing an expression of annoyance.

"JJ is trying to reach you. Also, I have a missed call from Nonna, too. But call JJ first. She's already threatened to cut off various parts of my anatomy if I don't stop hoarding you."

Even as exhausted as she was, it made Lucia smile. Noah was such a badass to everyone else but even he was a little scared of JJ. She made a mental note to mention it to her bestie since she'd definitely get a kick out of knowing she scared grown men. In JJ's mind that would be the ultimate compliment.

Lucia sat up. "Sorry, it's my fault. I've been avoiding

her calls because I wasn't sure what to say. Is it safe to tell her what's going on? I'm not putting her in danger if I confide in her, am I?"

"I think that train has already left the station. Call her. Please."

Lucia sighed. She knew he was right. It was way too late to worry about keeping JJ in the dark when she'd told her friend everything previously. Before she could overthink it, she grabbed her phone from the nightstand. Sure enough, she had several missed calls and two from Nonna. She really needed to call her back so she wouldn't worry. But first she hit the speed dial for JJ's number. Her friend answered immediately and the warm familiarity of her voice was like being enveloped in a warm hug. Lucia was startled by the rush of emotion that brought tears to her eyes.

"Hey, it's me."

"So, you finally decided to call me back. You shady bitch!"

Lucia laughed and pressed the back of her hand against her eyelids, holding the tears and the emotion away. "Noah made me. It turns out that he's pretty attached to whatever part of his anatomy you keep threatening to cut off."

JJ snorted. "Aren't they all? Babies, all of them. But

that's not why I've been calling. Happy birthday!"

Shock had Lucia pulling back from the phone and hitting the calendar app so she could check the date. What? It was her birthday. How could she have forgotten that? She closed her eyes. That must be why Nonna had called twice already. Every year she insisted on singing to Lucia and baking her a cake. She'd been floating in a fog for days now, sick with worry about Rafe, where he'd been and why he'd come back now. Personal things, even something that she'd been anticipating for ages, could easily slip anyone's mind when under this kind of stress. Which also explained why Noah had forgotten. She almost wished she could hide it from him. He would be so hard on himself for forgetting but she couldn't blame him. They had life or death things to focus on right now.

"I had forgotten, believe it or not."

"You forgot your birthday? But you've been talking about it all year. Hell, I've been talking about it all year." JJ's voice lowered until it was just above a whisper. "What is going on with you?"

"There are so many things I need to tell you. Things have been more than a little crazy around here lately."

"Well, you can tell me tonight after you buy me a margarita. I'm totally excited now that I don't have to get drinks for you anymore. Just kidding."

"No you're not."

JJ laughed. "No, I'm definitely not. Now we just have to figure out how to get your warden on board with the plan. He's keeping you locked up like a prisoner."

Lucia's thoughts went to her brother, back from the dead and with questionable motives. If JJ knew that Rafe was not only alive but had been in their office only a few feet from her, she wouldn't make fun of how vigilant Noah was being.

He would never hurt me. Would he?

It was painful to think of her brother as a potential enemy but she couldn't relax her guard. She'd asked him what he was doing and he hadn't been able to give her a straight answer. Which no doubt meant that he knew she wouldn't approve of whatever his plan was. Lucia was suddenly very afraid that whatever Rafe was planning would tear her away from Noah. Suddenly she wanted to see him. Needed to feel him in her arms one more time to make sure he knew they were real.

"Maybe I should just stay in tonight. With things the way they are, I'm not sure ... "

"Lucia, seriously?" JJ interrupted. "You're really not going to celebrate your birthday. Your *twenty-first* birthday?

Unashamed

No way, we are going out and getting you drunk."

"Somehow I don't think that's what I need right now. Noah would hit the roof."

"Contrary to popular opinion, Noah doesn't control the world," JJ muttered.

Lucia hated feeling like this. She'd never been the type of girl who ditched her friends for a guy and didn't want to start now. It probably seemed that way to JJ, like she was changing now that she'd hooked up with Noah finally, and the thought was all she needed to change her mind. Bad things were happening and there was nothing she could do about that. However, she could control how she responded to those things. Her response wasn't going to be hiding away and putting her head in the sand.

No doubt she was going to have to argue with Noah to convince him that it was safe but she didn't even care. What was the point of hiding in the house? Rafe had already proven that he wasn't averse to breaking in to get to her. So staying home was probably counterproductive anyway.

"You know what? You're right!"

"I am?" JJ said slowly.

"You are. It's my birthday and I'm going out. We

are going to have fun and … whatever. I'm not entirely sure on the details yet but I can't sit at home on my birthday."

"You're damn right you're not. Yay! Okay, so I'll figure out where we're going and then I'll let you know so you can clear it with the goons. I don't care if they come with us. Hell, I'll get them drunk too. We're going to have so much fun."

Her enthusiasm was contagious and Lucia found herself excited about the prospect of an adventure. She would probably have a whole slew of bodyguards on her like body lotion while she danced, but at least she wouldn't be at home feeling sorry for herself. She could only hope that Rafe wouldn't do anything crazy like try to kidnap her while she was out.

Or maybe he would. Lucia sat up, the idea taking root.

It felt treacherous to even think about it. Noah was so worried about her and working so hard to ensure her safety that she felt like a total Judas secretly wishing to see Rafe again. But now that she'd had the thought, she couldn't deny that she was hoping he would try to make contact with her. If she could only talk to him again maybe he would see reason. She could convince him to stop working against Noah and instead work with them. Clearly Rafe knew things that they didn't and despite what Noah thought, she couldn't believe her brother would ever actually hurt her.

"We are definitely going to have fun. I'll have Noah send someone to pick you up and we can get ready here." Belatedly, she realized how presumptuous she was being. Maybe JJ would have preferred to get ready at home. "Sorry, I'm just thinking that Noah will want us where he can protect us."

"It's okay; I get it. The big lug is protective of you. I like that, you know? He really loves you, Lucia. I know I give him a lot of shit but the two of you together, it's a good thing."

"Thanks. I like us together too."

"And tonight you are finally going to tell me the real deal about what's going on with you lately. Because I'm your bestie and you know you can't fool me. You haven't been yourself for weeks."

"I know. You'll get the full scoop tonight, I promise. Although once you find out everything you might wish you'd never asked."

JJ was quiet for a minute and then said, "No matter what you tell me, you know I have your back, right? The only thing I care about is making sure you're okay.

Whatever it is, we'll deal with it the way we always have. Together."

It made Lucia smile remembering how many scrapes and tight spots JJ had helped her scheme her way out of. But those things had been childish dilemmas, not life or death situations. There was a part of her that wished she didn't have to involve her friend in all these crazy shenanigans but if the tables were turned, she'd want JJ to trust in her.

"Yeah, together. And it's probably good that I'm twenty-one now because we are definitely going to need alcohol for this conversation."

Lucia walked away from the bar slowly, careful not to spill the drinks. The very first drinks she'd ever bought legally. It had been a weird thing to just walk up to the bar and order something. The times they went out, JJ always got the drinks since Lucia hadn't been old enough. Not that she was much of a drinker anyway. Mainly she'd just gone along to keep JJ company and to get herself out of the house.

Unashamed

She'd always been a bit of a loner, happy to lose herself in a fashion magazine with a hot cup of tea beside her. JJ often teased her that she was the only thing keeping Lucia from turning into an old maid.

Thinking about the things Noah had done to her before they left the house, Lucia figured her friend was no longer the only thing keeping her from being old before her time. Noah hadn't even cared that the others were in the living area waiting for them! The man was a menace. He truly had no shame. The only reason he'd stopped was Nonna calling again.

JJ accepted the drink Lucia handed her and then raised it in the air for a toast. "To my sister from another mister. Happy birthday, Lucia!"

Lucia had to laugh at the creative toast. "*Aww*. I love you, too. Cheers!"

JJ took a sip of her drink and then wiggled in delight. "Ooh, that's good."

Lucia took a sip of her own drink and had to agree. She had decided to go for something different in honor of her birthday and ordered them mojitos instead of doing shots. The sugary drink was exactly what she needed. Considering the mood JJ was in, she'd probably need the sugar in order to keep up.

When they'd arrived at the bar, she'd expected Noah to crowd them and hover like he usually did. To her surprise, he'd found a table for them and then retreated to stand against the wall on the other side of the room. Ryan was in the crowd somewhere, but she'd only seen him once. It was comforting and strange at the same time to know that they were out there watching her every move.

Her hand went to the delicate necklace resting between her breasts. After her conversation with JJ, she'd teased Noah about forgetting her birthday. It turned out he hadn't forgotten at all but was just planning a special dinner for her. She'd felt bad about ruining his dinner plans but he hadn't seemed to mind. He'd given her a carefully wrapped box instead which held the necklace she was now wearing. Even though he'd given her a lot of birthday gifts over the years, Lucia knew she'd always remember this one. Maybe it was because this was the first gift she'd gotten from him after knowing that he loved her.

"Okay so what's the deal? You've been acting so weird all night. What did He-Man do this time?"

Lucia snorted at JJ's never-ending litany of creative nicknames for Noah. Knowing his ego, he'd probably like the He-Man moniker.

"For the first time ever, it's not about Noah. I've

been having a hard time … remembering things about when my brother died."

JJ paused with her drink halfway to her mouth. They rarely talked about the dark period surrounding Rafe's death. That was one of the benefits of having a longtime friend: you didn't have to explain certain things because they'd been there. JJ knew how lost and inconsolable she'd been for years afterward. She didn't ask questions about that time because she'd been right in the thick of it with Lucia.

"I'm so sorry, Lu. Of course you'd be thinking about your brother right now. You're an adult and it must be so hard to go through all these milestones without him here."

JJ was quiet for a moment and when Lucia glanced over at her, she was shocked to see tears in her friend's eyes. JJ was the ball buster, the brash, loud, fearless friend that she relied on to push her boundaries and challenge the status quo. She'd only ever seen JJ cry from frustration or anger. Even when her feelings were hurt, she defaulted to rage instead of sorrow. But there was no mistaking that these were genuine tears of sadness.

"You're crying," she finally said, feeling stupid for stating the obvious but still in shock to see her friend so undone. In that moment, she was able to step outside of herself and realize how hard it must have been on JJ to watch her going through all these things over the years. It would be heartbreaking on her end if something horrible happened to JJ and there was nothing she could do to help.

JJ pressed her fingers below her eyes, pressing the skin as if determined to use sheer force of will to stop any tears from actually falling.

"Of course I'm crying. I'm a shitty friend. All you've been saying is that you need time and want to be alone while I'm here dragging you out for drinks. All because I feel like we're drifting apart and that scares me. This whole time I've been worrying about me instead of thinking about what you're going through."

Lucia put her hand over JJ's on top of the table. Her friend smiled and flipped her hand over to clasp hers tightly.

"First of all, you are not a shitty friend. You're the best friend I've ever had. The only person in the world that I could tell that—" She stopped before blurting out that Rafe was alive again. You never knew who was listening. "—certain things without you assuming I was crazy. I don't know what I'd do without you."

The relief on her friend's face made Lucia feel incredibly guilty. She hadn't realized how abandoned JJ had felt during this whole thing. If the roles were reversed, she'd probably feel the same way, but she'd never had to experience that because JJ had never put her boyfriends above their friendship.

"And I appreciate that you dragged me out tonight. Don't ever let me get so boring that I sit at home on my birthday, okay?"

By the appreciative way that JJ squeezed her hand, she knew her friend was happy to take their conversation to a lighter place. Neither of them had ever been the overly mushy type and if they kept up this line of conversation they might as well be at home watching sad movies and eating ice cream.

"You got it, babe. Speaking of not being boring, let's dance!"

Lucia tossed back the last of her drink while JJ did the same and then followed her friend to the dance floor. Noah wasn't anywhere around but she knew he still had eyes on her; that was a given. But without seeing him it was easier to close her eyes and get lost in the music.

This is what I need. To forget everything and just be.

JJ danced around her, all loose hips and sinuous arm movements. Lucia would never be able to dance like that; her friend had more sexiness in her pinkie finger than she had in her whole body, but under the influence, she let the rhythm of the music roll through her. For one night, she could forget all her problems and just do what felt good.

Then she opened her eyes and jumped slightly. Rafe danced next to them, looking for all the world like he belonged in a nightclub.

Before she could say anything, he put his finger over his lips. She nodded and then glanced at JJ who was staring at Rafe like he was … well, like he was a ghost. Without his businessman disguise, there was no doubt as to his identity. He motioned with his head for them to follow him. He moved through the crowd easily, people parting as he walked like he was some kind of messiah. Lucia glanced over her shoulder to find JJ following behind with a dazed expression on her face.

"It's okay. Trust me."

JJ nodded and grabbed her hand. Together they navigated the crowd until they finally reached a set of stairs that led to the rooftop bar. It was usually roped off for VIP guests but strangely, it was completely empty.

As soon as Rafe turned around, Lucia threw herself into his arms. "Where have you been?"

From this position, she could see JJ standing off to the side, watching them with wide eyes and a what-the-fuck expression.

"It doesn't matter where I've been. What matters is that I'm here now, and I'm never leaving you again." Rafe's words made her heart leap and then crash.

"Easy for you to say it doesn't matter," she mumbled.

His soft chuckle was at once so familiar that her knees buckled slightly. How many times had she heard that laugh, something he seemed to do only for her? It was a sound she'd thought never to hear again in this life. Her arms tightened around his neck until she must have been strangling him but he didn't protest, just rested his head on top of hers.

And for that moment, he was right. Nothing else mattered.

Chapter Ten

"Jesus, Lulu, I've missed you."

When Lucia looked up at her brother, all she wanted to do was hold him. "I missed you too." She looked down at her feet, shoving her hands in her back pockets. "My life was never the same after. My whole world fell apart when you were gone."

He reached for her and stroked his thumb over her cheek. "You have to understand. If there was any other way, I never would've left."

She frowned up at him. "Then tell me what happened. Why did you leave? What was so important that you had to go to that house? Do you know that for years I wasn't able to remember what happened?"

"Lulu, that's not something you have to worry about anymore. I'm back."

"All due respect, Rafe, but I do have to worry about it. You've shown back up in my life, and you expect me to just trust you blindly. When I needed you, you weren't here. Now that I'm able to stand on my own, you want to tell me I can't trust the man that I love." She threw her hands up. "You're going to have to give me more than that. I need more to go on."

Rafe ran his hand through his hair and stepped

back. "You don't think I want to tell you? You don't think I want to give you every reason to run away from him? The problem is the more you know, the more danger you're in. I've exposed myself coming for you. But there was no way I was going to let them hurt you. The people Noah works for, they're dangerous. They're ruthless. And they wouldn't hesitate to kill you just for knowing that I'm alive. I've stayed hidden a long time just to keep you safe. That's why I need to take you with me, get you to safety."

She shook her head. "You don't need to get me to safety. I'm safe with Noah."

"No, you're not. I don't know what game he's playing considering it's his organization that is hell-bent on killing you. Maybe he wants to hold you for information. Either way, it's not safe for you. I was able to get to you in that penthouse. Imagine what a horde of them could do. This isn't some little security company that plays at doing the right thing. Blake Security is a front. All of those guys in there, killers. That one guy, with the knife. Did you see the way he was enjoying it? He wanted to kill me. But he didn't want to make it quick. He wanted me to hurt. He wanted to enjoy himself. Those are the kind of people you're protecting? Those are the kind of people that you call friends?"

Unashamed

"You don't know anything about it. Because you weren't here."

He stared at her, pain evident in his eyes and the tight set of his lips. "I wanted to be."

"Not good enough. Not good enough by miles. And you just turn up at my office one day, no warning, no nothing. And you expect me to leave with you. Are you insane?"

He tossed his head back. "Clearly. Because if I had my way, I would just sedate you and carry you out of here. But you had to pick somewhere really fucking public. Let me guess: Noah's guys are posted at the exits? There's no safe way to take you out of here unless you can walk on your own. Too many innocent people could get hurt."

"You mean like my friends? Matthias and Jonas? Heads up, you could have permanently blinded him."

Her brother shrugged. "If the enemy can't see you, they can't kill you."

"For the love of God, they are not the enemy. They help people."

"Is that what Noah told you?"

She stared at him. That familiar face, but yet, somehow, unfamiliar. "Yes, that's what he told me. But it's also what I see. When some woman walks in there because she has a stalker ex-boyfriend and they make that stalker stop, I see that. I see the good that they're doing."

Rafe stepped into her space, staring down at her. When he spoke, his voice was low, and icy. "Just how do you think they make that stalker boyfriend stop? Do you think they have a stern conversation with him? Do you think they file a restraining order? They take that stalker ex-boyfriend, and they make him go away. Permanently."

"You're wrong. They don't kill people. Noah doesn't do that anymore. Besides, isn't this a case of the pot calling the kettle black? He told me that you trained him. You're as much of a killer as he is. Why would I trust you?"

"Because I'm your goddamned brother."

Lucia stepped back. "You'll have to do better than that."

Rafe scrubbed his hand over his face. "Yes, I did train him. And there was a time that the organization we worked for did good things. They took out the worst of the worst. And I was part of that. Those people that trafficked children and drugs and wanted to see whole populations decimated, those were the kinds of people we went after. But somewhere along the line, something changed; they became the people we were trying to stop. I saw it, found a

Unashamed

way out. And I took it. Noah, he never left."

"Yes, he did."

"No, he didn't. He's still in touch with them. How do you think he found out about the hit on you? He's still in bed with those people. And I need to get you away from him."

Lucia gasped.

JJ put her arm around her shoulders protectively. "Stop trying to scare her," she growled.

Rafe looked between them in frustration. "She needs to be scared. I'm trying to get her to see reason."

Lucia squeezed her friend's hand. JJ was worried about her, but she didn't want her friend getting in the middle of all of this. She didn't think Rafe would hurt her friend but that was the thing, she wasn't really sure what he would do now.

"You need to make me go willingly, and I'm not leaving him. You need to talk to him. Work out your differences; figure out what the hell is going on. Because there was a time when the two of you were on the same side."

"That time was a long time ago. Noah and I have nothing to say to each other."

143

"Just talk to him. I can set it up. It'll be okay. And at the very least, you can stop trying to hurt each other. You're both my family."

"He's not your family. I am."

"Well, you know what, Rafe? You abandoned me and he took over as family. Who the hell do you think has been looking after me and Nonna all this time? Making sure that Nonna had money to pay for things like my prom, like college?"

He took her by the shoulders "I did. I sent her money every month to make sure that you had what you needed."

Lucia's jaw dropped open and she staggered back a step, but her brother held onto her tightly. "What did you say?"

"I sent her money. Every damn month. I made sure she was taken care of. I made sure you were taken care of."

"Noah has been there for the Sunday dinners. He's been there when some idiot broke up with me and hurt me. Noah has been there. When Nonna started having health issues, he was there, helping me take her to the hospital and getting her checked up on. Bringing doctors over. Where were you?"

"Lucia, I was always watching from afar, making

sure you would be okay. I was never far away."

"Oh yeah, you think that counts for anything? What I needed was someone who was here. To help me carry the burden."

"Look, you don't understand. And you won't. Not for a while. Because he's pretty much got you brainwashed. If you just come with me, I can get you help. Get you away, and then you can see things clearly."

"I'm not going with you Rafe."

And then a mask slid over her brother's face. Cold and efficient. And suddenly she could see the killer he must've been. "Yes, you are Lucia. Even if I have to knock you out and drag you out of here. I have one other exit. It's not ideal, but I can take you unconscious."

The next three seconds happened so quickly she didn't understand what was going on at first. It took her a moment to catalog everything. Suddenly, Rafe's hands were off her shoulders and he was fighting with Matthias.

Oh God. Next to her, on one side stood Ryan, his gun trained on her brother. On her other side stood Dylan, in the same position. His gun was ready and trained on the fighting duo, safety off. Oskar, Jonas and Noah watched as Matthias unleashed on Rafe.

"Stop it," she screamed. But either they couldn't hear her, or they didn't care. Either way, they were going after it. Elbows crunched noses, arms got dragged behind them. She heard cracking noises. She shuddered, knowing that bones were breaking.

What she saw terrified her. Dylan, Ryan, Noah, Jonas, and Oskar all just watched calmly as Matthias and her brother fought. And Rafe was right. Matthias looked like this was a good time. The problem was so did Rafe. Their expressions were identical as they fought.

With a flurry of kicks, Rafe was pushed back toward her. Ryan and Dylan stepped in front of her to shield her, and she tried to see around their massive shoulders. Damn it. She scooted around Dylan and stood on tiptoes look around his shoulder. "Stop. Please, you'll hurt him. Rafe, I swear to God if you hurt Matthias…" She felt like a girl watching a schoolyard fight.

The two shifted again, prowling around each other, and finally Noah put up a hand.

"Okay, that's enough Matthias. You got it out of your system. Anyone else have anything you need to say to Rafe?"

"I've got a bullet with his name on it," said Oskar.

A bullet? Hell no. It was one thing when Noah

asked her to wear a wire to try and convince Rafe to talk to them. It was another thing if Rafe was going to get hurt. Lucia shoved against Dylan, who she caught off guard so he actually managed to shift enough so she stepped around him, sprinting to her brother before stepping directly in front of him.

"No. No one else I care about is going to get hurt tonight. So all of you put your guns down. Now!"

"Lucia, get away from him!" Noah reached out, as if he could pull her to safety even from a distance. But before he could move, she saw Rafe's arm come up.

And in the span of a few seconds, Lucia went from peacemaker to hostage.

Noah stared at the man who had been his mentor. It really was him.

He knew from the surveillance footage that the guy in Lucia's office looked like Rafe. But to see him fight, to see him holding a gun on the woman he loved, Noah knew it was him, the man he'd once called his brother.

Where the hell had he been? All this time—as the guilt had wracked Noah and the sorrow had torn Lucia apart—Rafe had been alive. But where? What the hell had happened?

"Rafe, you can understand my surprise in seeing you, you know, alive and shit."

"Sorry to disappoint you Noah."

"Disappoint me?" Noah shifted on his feet. His eyes tracked the gun pressed to Lucia's side.

Would Rafe really do it? Would he shoot his own sister? *If he thinks he's saving her life. If he thinks he's saving her from you.* Just how fucked-in-the-head was Rafe right now?

"I mean, dude, you did me a favor. I carried a lot of guilt around. But you're alive and well, so now I can feel free to be my usual shameless self."

"Nothing's changed for you Noah, still too cocky. You still think you know everything."

"I will admit I did *not* know this. You can imagine my surprise when the friend I buried walked into his sister's office."

Rafe narrowed his gaze. "We gonna stand around all night, or are we going to fight?"

Unashamed

Noah looked at his men. All of them with kill shots. None of them moving. Especially not Matthias. He had his killer face on. The one that remained detached and unemotional, and didn't give two shits. At a time like this, that was the face Noah needed. They'd all pay for it later though.

Noah did the one thing that Rafe wouldn't expect. He reached around his waist, and pulled the Velcro for his bulletproof vest off. When he slid his arms through and tugged it over his head, he tossed it to the ground. And then he de-armed himself. Tossed the gun in the holster at his back, tossed his ankle piece, and he tossed the one he was holding. He also rid himself of the knives. *Almost* all of them anyway. That was saying something.

Rafe frowned. "What are you doing?"

"What was that thing that pirates used to do? When they wanted to have a conversation to see if it was really necessary to blow each other out of the water? I saw it in the *Pirates of the Caribbean* movie. Parlay?"

Rafe scoffed. "You think that's a real thing?"

Noah shrugged. "I'm not sure. But considering Lucia has put herself in harm's way to save your life, I figure you're worth having a conversation with before I let my guys kill you for real. And I'd rather you point that gun somewhere other than your sister. You want to shoot something, shoot me."

"My *sister* doesn't seem to know what's best for her. So if I have to convince her, then so be it."

From the periphery of his vision, Noah saw Jonas's eye twitch. And he prayed that twitch was a result of what the toxin had done and not an emotional response. If Jonas was going to get emotional, that meant trouble. Jonas was usually the coolheaded one. But when he had an emotional response, shit got out of control real quick. And Noah knew he wasn't the only one who loved Lucia. All the guys did. Any one of them would give their life to protect her. And he didn't need anyone getting all emotional and trigger-happy right now. They'd all come way too close to death lately.

"Even if it's not a real thing, it's got to be worth a shot. No one's dying today, Rafe. You seem to have a problem with me. And I get that."

Rafe shrugged "Well, you *did* shoot me dead."

"Is that how you remember it? I seem to remember you jumped in front of my bullet."

"Oh, Noah. Semantics. Either way, you shot me. Period."

"Yeah, about that, Rafe. We're even. Gotta say, seeing you back like this makes me real paranoid. Care to explain what the hell's going on?"

"What's going on is I'm trying to keep my sister alive."

"Okay, I feel like you're being deliberately obtuse, and you're missing the irony, seeing as you have a gun on her. I'll break it down. Who the hell do you work for?"

There was a long pause. Lucia slowly rotated in her brother's hold, giving her back to Noah. "It's a fair question, Rafe. One both Noah and I deserve the answer to."

Rafe sighed then clenched his jaw, but he didn't holster his weapon. "I work for the FBI. I've been an undercover agent for the past eleven years."

What the fuck? That was not what Noah was expecting. "So what, ORUS was doing some sort of exchange program?"

Rafe shook his head. "No. For years, ORUS was the government's dirty little secret. The group to do the kind of wet work even the CIA wasn't going to do. The government sent ORUS into the worst places. Gave them the hardest targets. And they got the job done. But at some point, someone in ORUS started making their own targets. When the Feds got wind of it, they needed a young recruit, someone to go in and infiltrate. A deep, deep cover assignment. At the same time, it offered me the ability to stay close to home. All I had to do was be me."

Lucia shook her head, completely in disbelief. "That's not true. If you had been in the FBI, I would've known about it."

"No. You wouldn't. I was recruited during my junior year of college. My entire training was centered around breaking into cells like these. Exposing the traitors and moving on. I came by my position in ORUS the good old-fashioned way. I worked my way in. A little padding of my mercenary resume, and I was recruited, just like the Feds wanted me to be." He nodded at Noah. "I'd been there a year when they assigned you to me."

Noah shook his head. *No.* "There were jobs. We took jobs. No Fed would be able to do that."

"We all do what we need to do to survive. The hits that I took, the hits that I let you take, they were legitimate kills. The one time I stopped you, you were about to kill an undercover FBI agent. Even if you were none the wiser, I didn't want them to come after you."

So it had been deliberate. "You worked with him?"

Rafe nodded. "He was undercover with the Del Tino crime family. We shared a handler. About a year into his assignment, we realized that many of ORUS's

Unashamed

assignments coincided with Del Tino hits. We were working both cases together when the job came in to take out a Del Tino lieutenant. Someone blew his cover and they sent you in to kill him."

Noah's stomach churned.

Rafe continued. "When I found out they sent you to make the kill, I couldn't let that happen; for his *and* your sake. Because if you'd done it, they would've hung you out to dry. It was a set up. So I took the hit."

The pent-up fury, grief, and anger from the last six years spilled forth. "You let us think you were dead. You let *her* think you were dead. Just so you could play undercover. What happened to the man I knew?"

Rafe shook his head. "You didn't know me. Just like I didn't know you. I thought after you murdered your mentor, you would be out of ORUS. But instead you're still doing their bidding."

Noah shook his head. "No. I left. After what happened to you, I couldn't stomach it. I couldn't sleep at night. So I left." He inclined his head toward Matthias. "Took him with me."

Rafe's brows drew up. "Orion allowed that?"

Noah shrugged. "He didn't have much of a choice. I

don't work for them anymore."

Rafe released the safety of his gun. "And here is where we reach an impasse. Because I know for a fact that you're in touch with Phoenix."

"He called, warning about the hit on your sister. That's it. As far as Phoenix is concerned, ORUS are still the good guys. He doesn't know what they are. Either that or he thinks it's too late to get out."

Rafe shook his head. "No. I know you're still in."

Lucia spoke up. "Rafe, I told you. Noah isn't lying. He's been out."

For the first time, Noah saw hints of his former mentor.

"The kind of surveillance you had at Lucia's place, I would have sworn you were still inside. I knew I had to get her away from you."

"I only added that extra security because they were coming for her. What was I supposed to do? Watch them kill the woman I love? Never going to happen."

Rafe stared at him. "You almost sound like you mean that."

Noah slid a glance to Lucia. "I do mean that."

Lucia reached a hand out for her brother's gun.

"Rafe, we have to start trusting each other at some point. We've all lied. All hurt each other. It has to stop. Because we're fighting the wrong people. The enemy of my enemy is my friend, right? These people will keep coming for me. We need to work together."

Rafe squared his shoulders. "I'm your brother. I'll protect you."

Noah shook his head. "She's mine. *I* protect her."

Lucia just rolled her eyes. "You two can stop posturing and marking your territory. I'm not having it. Right now we need solutions. If you're down for solutions, great. If not, we need to go."

Noah slid a glance to Rafe. "Maybe it is time to call a truce. We'll sort everything out as we go." He held out his hand.

For a long moment, Noah was pretty sure Rafe wouldn't take it. Then his once-mentor looked between him and Lucia and slowly took Noah's hand.

Chapter Eleven

Unashamed

Lucia hadn't thought a truce meant they'd all be friends, but she hadn't expected it to feel as dangerous as when they all had guns on each other either. She glanced around the living room of Blake Securities' new office with trepidation. Rafe stood on one side with her and JJ while Noah and the rest of the guys stood on the other. When she caught JJ's eye, her friend tried to smile but it came out more like a grimace.

I'm sorry, she mouthed. Once they'd decided they would talk, Noah had insisted that everyone be present. Apparently he didn't trust anyone to leave and possibly inform anyone else of their whereabouts. He'd loaded her and JJ in the van with him and Matthias and they'd all rode over in silence. She hadn't seen Rafe get out of a car but he'd ended up in the garage with them when they arrived. Clearly her brother had the silent but deadly ninja thing down pat.

"So maybe we should start with the most important thing," Noah began when no one else seemed inclined to speak. "Someone is trying to kill Lucia and you claim it isn't you."

Rafe glowered. "Of course it's not me. I thought it was you. I've been trying to get her away from you to keep her safe."

"I've spent the last six years trying to keep her safe in your memory. Why would I kill her now?"

"Orders. Greed. Because you're a sonofabitch. How the hell should I know?" Rafe crossed his arms.

"I am but she makes me better," Noah countered.

Lucia softened hearing Noah's gruffly muttered declaration of love. With a man like him, this was the equivalent of him taking out a billboard to announce it to the whole city. JJ nudged her in the side with her elbow and Lucia finally let go of the smile she'd been holding back.

"God, this is ridiculous. You've got my baby sister shacked up here with you and smiling like some lovesick airhead."

"Hey, that is unnecessary," JJ cut in.

Jonas glared at her. "Maybe don't antagonize the psycho who could decide to switch sides and kill us all at any moment, hmm?"

"Hey, he wasn't gunning for me, big guy. Maybe Lucia and I should just step aside and let you all fight it out."

Jonas looked like he wanted to say something else but Lucia held up a hand to stop the conversation.

"This isn't helping anything. None of this stuff really matters. I don't believe that my brother was gone for years only to come back to kill me. That doesn't make any sense."

Rafe smiled at her. "Glad to see you haven't completely lost your mind lately."

"Oh no. You don't get off so easily," Lucia jabbed him in the chest with her finger. JJ's gasp behind her would have been funny in any other situation. They were all treating Rafe like a ticking time bomb, but once it had sunk in that it was truly Rafe, her big brother, her defender, she wasn't afraid of him.

How could she be afraid of him when she remembered him holding her after she had a nightmare? Rafe was the one who'd told her not to let mean girls or clueless boys get her down. He'd told her that she was special and that she could be a fashion designer if she wanted. That she could do anything.

And she'd known it was true because she'd have her big brother helping her no matter what.

"You don't get to just show up out of nowhere and pretend like nothing has happened. You died, Rafe." Her voice broke slightly on the last word, and for the first time she saw a crack in his stark exterior and a little bit of the brother she remembered peeked through.

With a muffled curse, he grabbed her and hugged her. Although she heard Noah and the guys behind her shouting, she didn't care. She clung to him just like she had when she was a little girl. And when his hand landed on the back of her head, the heavy weight of it both familiar and foreign, it felt like her world was breaking apart.

"I never should have left you. Should have taken you and Nonna with me, we could have run together." Rafe sounded almost as tortured as she felt.

"Why didn't you? You just left us. How could you do that?"

"I didn't want that life for you, Lulu. Never that. You deserved so much more. I thought I could watch over you from afar and then you could have all the things you'd dreamed about. Going to design school and having your own fashion company. I wanted that for you."

Lucia sobbed against his neck, not even listening at this point. She heard what he was saying, but didn't he know those things hadn't mattered once he'd gone? She'd rather have had her beloved brother a million times over than anything else.

"Don't leave me again. Promise me."

When she pulled back, she was shocked as hell to see tears on her brother's face as well. He blew out a breath before glancing over at the others. She turned too and found the whole group staring at them. Noah didn't exactly look happy and she knew there would be a lecture coming later about not trusting Rafe so easily, but she didn't care.

She had her brother back.

"I'm not leaving this time, I promise. I'm going to find a way to end this thing for good. It's the only way you'll be safe."

Noah finally spoke up. "Any ideas about how to do that?"

"A few. Are you going to trust me to execute without slipping a knife in your back?"

Lucia tensed in his arms, and Rafe glanced down at her with a slightly annoyed look on his face. It was so him, so pre-tragedy Rafe, that despite the seriousness of the situation she laughed.

"Threats of violence make you laugh now? Maybe you have been good for her." Rafe glanced over at Noah, and after the longest, tensest pause ever, extended his hand.

Lucia could almost feel everyone else in the group let out a collective sigh of relief. The men might not like each other or trust each other but they'd work together. For now.

"I don't think there's any doubt that she is the one who has been good for me," Noah said as he accepted the handshake.

Rafe smiled again but this time, it looked predatory. "Finally something we can agree on. Now let's get to work."

Noah watched Rafe leave with a sinking feeling. Correction, he watched *Lucia* watch Rafe leave with a sinking feeling. Her eyes followed her brother's form as if she was afraid she'd never see him again. A valid fear, all things considered.

"My brother's really alive," she whispered.

Noah wasn't sure if she knew she'd spoken aloud, but he'd had just about enough of talking about Rafe. It was so odd to go from thinking of him as a friend and mentor to a potential enemy, but there was no other option to consider when Lucia's life was on the line.

He believed Rafe when he said he hadn't been trying to hurt her. His only concern at this point was whether Rafe might put Lucia in danger inadvertently trying to achieve his goal. Whatever that was. They'd hashed out quite a bit but the one thing Rafe had made sure to avoid was his current status; if he was still undercover with the FBI, what was he working on and did it relate to ORUS in any way? So many questions and Rafe had always been a secretive bastard. They wouldn't get anything out of him unless he wanted them to.

However, there was one thing Noah knew for sure; Rafe loved Lucia. People changed, sure, but not that much. The old Rafe had structured his entire world around the little sister who he loved more than his own heartbeat. Six years wouldn't change that.

"Yes, he is. And we're going to figure this all out. Rafe will work on his contacts and we'll continue to do everything we can to keep you safe. I might be out of ORUS but that doesn't mean we don't still have our ways of keeping tabs on them."

Lucia leaned against his chest, taking Noah by surprise. She'd been standoffish, cold, since they'd gotten home. She was annoyed that he'd made her wear the wire and then even more annoyed that he'd used it to ambush her brother. But this one simple action showed him that all was right in their world. Or it would be.

Eventually.

"Promise you'll be careful. I made Rafe promise not to leave me again but I need you to do the same thing. Despite what you think, I need you just as much Noah. When Rafe died … when we thought he'd died, it was the worst pain I could imagine. But I survived."

She stood back and looked him in the eye as she spoke and Noah had never been more fucking proud of her. This was no scared little girl; his princess was a survivor. Beautiful, strong and stubborn as hell. God, he loved her. She put her hands on his face, bringing his attention back to her words.

"I survived because I had you. You were the one who kept me anchored. That's always been you, my port in the storm. But if anything ever happened to you, I don't think I'd survive it."

Just like that she fucking slayed him, absolutely tore his heart out with her sweet words and those big, beautiful eyes that saw straight through to his soul. This woman was his everything and for her, he'd do the impossible. He, Noah no-name Blake, who'd always been only two steps ahead of a bullet at any time, would live forever. He'd cheat the Reaper; he'd say however many Hail Marys it took; but he wasn't leaving Lucia alone in this world.

There were going to be quite a few things he'd have

to accomplish to give her that peace of mind but somehow, he'd make it happen.

"Nothing is going to happen to any of us. I'll make sure of it."

Lucia didn't look convinced but she didn't press the issue. Instead she wrapped her arms around him in a quick hug and then glanced behind her where JJ was making uncomfortable conversation with Jonas.

"Now I need to have a long overdue conversation with my best friend. I think she deserves some explanations after being held against her will for the past hour."

Noah observed the body language going on between Jonas and JJ. They both looked pissed but … intrigued. Oh no. The last thing he needed was a member of his team getting freaky with Lucia's best friend. He'd be right in the middle of the drama if anything went wrong, and he had no patience for that. He made a mental note to tell Jonas to sniff elsewhere as soon as he could get him alone.

"Good luck with that," he said finally.

While Lucia walked over to talk to her friend, Matthias approached with a smug look on his face. Noah had only seen that look a few times, so whatever the kid wanted to tell him was probably going to be good.

"Why do you look like you just got finished creating the perfect computer wife?"

Matthias scowled. "I have good news, actually."

"You put a tracker on Rafe?"

"No. I wish. None of us can get close enough to the bastard to even try that." Matthias touched his jaw absently, probably remembering what happened the first time he'd tried. "I was able to access information from the time period in question."

"Do I even want to know how many laws you broke to do that?"

"Not really. Anyway, everything supports Rafe's story. All signs point to him being an agent, although I can't tell which agency. Maybe CIA?"

Finally something was going their way. Noah took a deep breath. He'd made promises to Lucia. But even though she'd be pissed if she found out he was investigating her brother, it was necessary. He would rather have her angry than hurt. Besides, hopefully she'd never have to know. As long as Rafe was telling them the truth, Noah was happy to work with him if it meant Lucia was protected.

"At least he was honest about that," he mumbled.

Matthias laughed. "You know, as weird as this is going to sound, it was kind of nice to actually talk to him when he *wasn't* trying to kill me. The dude is a beast with the hand to hand. I've never seen anyone move so fast."

Noah laughed too. After all the tension lately, it was good to have something to smile about again. Only Matthias would think it was fun to talk to a guy who'd beaten him to hell.

"He was a legend in ORUS. Even if I'd been paired with him for twenty years I don't think I could have learned everything he had to teach."

"Well, now you can. Seems like everyone's getting a do-over, huh?" With those words of wisdom, Matthias walked off, leaving Noah thinking about possibilities.

Chapter Twelve

Unashamed

"Let me guess: you're mad."

Lucia turned to Noah and shrugged. "Oh, you think I'm mad?" She unhooked her earrings and slid them into her jewelry box before turning to face him. "First, you had me wired and I didn't know it."

"Lucia, you agreed to wear a wire."

"Yes. I did. But I thought I would have a say when that wire was going on." She unhooked her necklace and stared at it for a moment, then sighed. "Let me guess. This has a GPS tracker and a transmitter?"

At least, he had the good grace to look sheepish. "Look, once you said you were okay with wearing a wire, I had that made. I would've loved to give you advance warning, but there wasn't going to be time. And we had no way of knowing when Rafe was going to try and find you."

"So you thought he'd try on my birthday?"

Noah shrugged. "Well, before he died, he never missed one. Your whole family made birthdays a big deal. Plus, the club was crowded enough, had multiple exits, and is pretty hard to defend. If I were him, and I wanted to make a play for you, I would've chosen a place like that. So, sorry but it needed to be this way."

She planted her hands on her hips. "Fair enough. I

get why you couldn't wire me up the traditional way. But that doesn't explain why you didn't tell me. You gave me a gift. At least what I thought was a gift."

He frowned. "I'm sorry. I figured if you knew you would inadvertently draw attention to it. It's not like you're trained for these types of situations. People telegraph all kinds of things that they don't mean to. It was easier not to tell you."

She threw up her arms. "This is what I mean, Noah. We have had this conversation a million times. But you keep making decisions without consulting me. You don't give me the opportunity to do things on my own. To figure it out. It's like you don't trust me. And that hurts."

"Lulu, I trust you with my life. I've never had anybody love me before. And yes, I can certainly do better. Yes, I need to figure this shit out. I've never had a real relationship before. There are women I've dated for covers, there are women who were convenient, but I've never been with anyone I wanted to be with before. I have no idea what I'm doing."

The honesty in his eyes was her undoing. She didn't want to just let it go, but she knew how hard this was for him. "Well, trust is part of being with someone. We need to be partners. And I need to trust that you're not going to spring some random shit on me."

"Can you maybe trust that if I do, there's a reason behind it? And not assume that I don't believe in you or that I'm just trying to fuck with you, or make your life more difficult? Or treat you like a child?"

She opened her mouth to retort, but he had a point. He was right. She and Noah had had that dynamic for so long, she also didn't know how to deal with him in the context of a relationship. "Okay, I can try to do that. We've just had a certain dynamic for a very long time."

He nodded. "Back then, my only job was to protect you. Not protect your feelings, not explain things to you, or check with you. But then, when everything started, that shifted. And it's hard for me to adjust. I'm sorry. I'll work harder on that."

She licked her lips, and then nodded. "I'm sorry too. Tonight was like exposing a raw wound."

"Yeah, tell me about. It was one thing to see him in video footage, but it was another thing entirely to see him in the flesh. After all this time. That's going to take a long time to get used to."

She chewed her bottom lip. "Do you really think he would've shot me?"

Noah laughed. "Absolutely. Somewhere nonlethal, probably more like a graze really. But it would've hurt, and you would've done what he wanted."

She winced. "My own brother would have shot me?"

Noah strode over and covered her hand with his. "He would've done it to protect you. Hell, I would've done it to protect you. If I could've shot you to get you out of the way, so that you didn't risk your life for him, I would've done it."

She lifted her eyes to meet his gaze. "Do not put me in the middle, Noah. Don't make me choose between you and Rafe. I can't do it. I love you both."

Noah's jaw worked. "You mean like he did with you?"

She jutted her chin out. "And I chose you. I wasn't willing to leave you. And I'm not willing to let anyone hurt him. Nor am I willing to let him hurt anyone else anymore. We're going to have to work together."

Noah nodded and stroked her cheek gently with his thumb. "Lucia, I promise you no one's going to get hurt. Except for the people that deserve it. We're on the same side. And just so we're clear, I've missed him too. He was my family too."

Her eyes stung and she rapidly blinked back the tears. "I know. You're okay though?"

"Yeah, I'm okay. Though …" He inched closer and slid his arms around her lower back. "I have some ideas on how you can help me feel better."

She couldn't help the giggle. "Why do I get the impression that if you had your way you'd forever keep me in this room naked?"

"Because that's a fabulous idea."

Noah wasted no time getting her naked. But then had Noah ever wasted time? Hell, half the time he didn't bother to even get her completely naked first.

His kiss was searing. His expert tongue sliding into her mouth, claiming her and with each stroke making her burn. His big hands slid over her heated flesh and Lucia sizzled with each caress. Would she ever get enough of this?

Lucia rocked her hips upward and reached for him, sliding her fingers though his hair. "Please hurry."

Noah understood the art of seduction. Knew how to make her want. Knew the buttons to push to make her scream. Or to bring her so close and hold off just enough so she'd hang on the precipice of need. It was enough to make her crazy. Enough to make her beg for what she needed. She was addicted to him. There was no way this would ever be enough.

He had her just where he wanted her. He had her tank off in seconds, the silky material falling to the floor. They both kicked off their shoes. And then the race was on to see who could get naked the fastest.

Noah of course didn't have to contend with a pesky bra. But obviously he was more than ready and willing to help her with that.

As he slid the lace from her skin, his fingertips grazed her flesh slightly, making her need him, making her want to beg for his mouth on her. She couldn't help the whimper that escaped.

He picked her up, carrying her to the bed, his lips on hers. But while she was in a hurry, Noah … was not. He was in the mood to tease. He kissed down her sternum, refusing to kiss her just where she needed. Refusing to give her what she wanted.

With a frustrated growl, she narrowed her gaze at

him. He chuckled. "Something you need, princess? Because I was in the mind to take my time with you. And we're just getting started."

"Damn it, Noah. You know what I want. Why are you torturing me?"

"Don't worry. I'll get there," Noah said with a chuckle. He grazed along the column of her throat even as his hips rocked into hers, pressing gently. Teasing her with the ridge of his erection. "Just so you know, I'm going to use my fingers, I'll slide them inside you and over your flesh. I'll find your G-spot and touch it just right. Just enough to make you come again. I know you'll be sensitive, but it's going to feel so good."

He sped up his movements, his hips rolling into hers. She rose to meet him, arching her back, begging him to rub her where she needed. His lips skimmed over her skin, across her collarbone to her breast. His words alone were driving her nuts. But coupled with his lips, his hands intertwined with hers, she was ready to explode.

His lips brushed her nipple ever so slightly. The motion sent a spear of need directly to her core. Next, he used just his teeth, raking gently. He was careful to keep his full weight off of her. His teeth felt so good and she wondered if it was possible to die from anticipation.

When he laved her distended nipple with his tongue and then wrapped his lips around her, Lucia held on for her life. With tug after deep tug, he sucked on her. It didn't take much, she was so tightly wound. But it was the secondary pleasure when he teased her other nipple with his thumb that sent her over the edge. She came hard and fast, her whole body shaking. "Noah. Oh my God."

"That's one," he announced with a satisfied grin.

He kissed down her thighs and her calves before pulling back to snag a condom out of his wallet. Lucia watched with avid interest as he sheathed himself before settling between her thighs.

"Look at me," he growled.

As if she could look anywhere else. Even though she felt like a limp noodle, she still wanted more.

One hand teasing the hair at his nape, the other tracing his pecs, she canted her hips up. "Noah, hurry."

She could see the tension in him as his arms shook. He was having a hard time with control. Would talking to him drive him as crazy as it drove her? He lined his erection up with her opening and she whispered, "I want to know what this feels like bare. Just you and me, nothing between us. Do you think you'll like that?"

He stared down at her, lips slightly parted. "What?"

Unashamed

"It would be a first. I want to know what it feels like to have you come inside me."

He rocked into her in one deep stroke, her name on his tongue. He cursed low and deep, a long drawn out "*Fuuuuck*."

Noah slid in and retreated, adjusting their position so she sat on his lap. Oh yes, it was so deep like this. Their movements were a frenzy of skin, lips and hands. There wasn't a part of him he didn't touch her with. Body and soul.

Her second orgasm was stronger than the first but with a slow build. Once the fire took hold, there was no stopping it and she exploded in his arms. Noah was right behind her. His hips bucked as he came, gripping her ass tight as his muscles corded and his teeth clenched. Lucia wrapped her arms around him, holding tight.

He was hers.

Chapter Thirteen

Unashamed

The next morning, Noah set out everything he needed to cook the perfect birthday breakfast. She hadn't even seemed angry that he'd forgotten her birthday, but he'd apologized anyway. Despite everything happening, it appalled him that something so monumental could slip his mind. He never wanted to take her for granted or assume that she'd forgive him when he messed up. He'd woken up early and spent a long time just watching Lucia sleep. There in the quiet dark he'd been happier than he knew it was possible to be and it hit him. This was it. This was the dream. He had everything that some men spent their whole lives searching for.

Were things perfect? Not by a long shot. He scowled, remembering that at this very moment ORUS was probably reassigning Lucia's hit contract to another operative. But with Rafe working on their side, he was confident they could keep her safe until they found a way to neutralize ORUS for good.

It was probably hubris to assume he could handle the situation so easily but he'd done it once before. Everyone had told him that getting out was impossible but he'd done it. Not only had he negotiated release for himself, he'd also managed to finagle Matthias's freedom in the process. As he knew from that experience it was all about planning and amassing information to use against the powers that be. He'd gathered enough intel to threaten ORUS with exposure, and they'd had little choice but to allow him his freedom.

Somehow, some way, he'd do the same thing for Lucia.

He hummed to himself as the bacon sizzled in the pan next to him while he scrambled the eggs. Cooking wasn't something he was particularly good at, but this morning he paid extra attention to every step. The last few days hadn't exactly been the ideal birthday celebration but he was going to make up for that today. Lucia deserved the absolute best.

"Look at the little man, making breakfast for the lady of the house."

Noah startled at the sound of Rafe's voice behind him. "What the fuck? How the hell did you get in here?"

Matthias appeared behind him looking like he'd seen a ghost. He glanced between Noah and Rafe with trepidation. "I don't know what happened. He didn't show up on any of the cameras."

Noah hissed when he noticed the eggs had burned slightly. With a flick of his wrist, he turned off the burner. Hopefully he could just discard the edges and wouldn't have to start over.

"It's fine Matthias. I'm pretty convinced at this point that Rafe is actually a ghost sent here to torment us for our many sins."

The kid left muttering something about firewalls, and Noah turned his attention back to breakfast. He kept Rafe in the periphery of his vision at all times. It was Rafe and at one time he'd trusted him with his life, but a lot had happened since he'd been gone. For years, Noah had trusted no one. It was hard to change six years of habit.

"I'm making breakfast for Lucia. Her birthday celebration got a little fucked by all this stuff, and she deserves better. She deserves everything. And we're all going to make sure she gets it." Hopefully his pointed look conveyed the message that Rafe had better not do anything to interfere with Lucia's happiness.

For a long moment the two men stared each other down, each gauging the other's sincerity and intentions, until finally Rafe grinned.

"I always knew you had a thing for her."

It was so unexpected to see that smile after so long that Noah turned away and cleared his throat. Fuck, he'd missed the bastard.

"You wouldn't rather see her with someone else? Someone ... better than me?"

Noah would probably later be annoyed that he'd asked the question. The last thing he wanted to do was telegraph his insecurity to Rafe. If you'd asked him a few days ago whether he thought Rafe would have approved, he wouldn't have thought he cared so much. But it mattered ... a hell of a lot.

Rafe shrugged. "What, like an accountant or something? Some guy with good benefits who'll come home by six o'clock every night?"

"Yeah, someone like that."

"The kind of guy who won't understand what she's been through, who'll have a mid-life crisis at forty and cheat on her with some bitch who works in his office? A guy who can't protect her if we can't get this shit with ORUS settled?"

Noah swallowed. "I guess there's no normal for her after all this. She deserves so much more."

"She deserves a guy who'd kill for her."

Noah looked up in surprise at the approval in Rafe's voice.

"Don't look so surprised. I trained you; I'm a little biased. Besides, I don't have to worry about a mid-life crisis with you. Guys like us have been in crisis our whole lives. We've already learned how to deal with our shit."

Noah chuckled as he arranged a plate for them to share. Lots of eggs, four strips of bacon, fruit on the side. He poured a cup of coffee and then after a moment of hesitation poured another one for Rafe. When he slid it across the counter, the other man took it gratefully. They weren't one big happy family quite yet but it was a start.

"I'll go wake her up and then let her know you're here. She'll be really happy." Noah picked up the tray and walked down the hall toward the bedroom. He'd planned to keep her in bed all morning but seeing her brother would be the best birthday present she could ask for.

He set the tray next to her on the bed and then peppered her face with soft kisses. She rolled over and then blinked sleepily. Once she woke up, she wrapped her arms around his neck and pulled him down until he fell laughing on top of her.

After several slow, teasing kisses, Lucia glanced over at the tray on the other side of the bed. "You made me breakfast? That's so sweet."

"Well, things didn't go as planned yesterday so I wanted a do-over. Happy birthday, princess."

She giggled and reached over to snag a piece of bacon. "I like do-overs. And I love bacon. But even I don't think I can eat all of this."

"Oh, don't worry. I plan to help you." He took a bite of the bacon she held out to him. His soft laughter warmed her all over.

After they'd worked their way through most of the plate, he put the tray on the night table.

"We're going to Nonna's later for dinner but right now, I have a surprise for you. So you'll need to get dressed, which makes me wonder why I'm giving you this gift since I'd prefer you take clothes off instead of put them on."

Lucia squealed and shot off the bed. He watched in amusement as she struggled to get into the jeans she'd discarded beside the bed the night before. She turned in a circle looking for a shirt before giving up and getting one from the dresser.

"I'm ready. Let's go!"

Noah chuckled. "I forgot how much you love surprises. You're like a little kid at Christmas."

"Hurry up!" Lucia yanked at his hand playfully before racing out the door. He knew the exact moment when she found her brother because she squealed again.

When he found them in the living room, Lucia was

wrapped up in Rafe's arms. Their eyes met over her brother's shoulder and even from across the room he could read the words she mouthed.

Thank you.

Lucia glanced over at her brother for the millionth time and smiled. She looked away before he caught her staring again. He was so different now, hard and remote in a lot of ways but underneath all that, she could still feel her Rafe, the one who'd make silly faces to make her smile or take her to Coney Island to cheer her up.

She hadn't really believed it before; it had seemed like a dangerous thing to trust that her brother was really back in her life. But he was here, standing in the living room with all her nearest and dearest looking like he belonged. Even Oskar had stopped giving him the hairy eyeball, although he did rub his shoulder absently every time Rafe was near.

It was going to take time, she thought. They wouldn't adjust to the new way of things overnight, but she was starting to believe that she could really have it all. Noah, her friends and Rafe, all a part of her life. It was almost like things were going back to the way they would have been if that horrible day six years ago had never happened.

Then she thought about the destruction at Noah's old office, being terrorized in her apartment and poor Brent, who'd never done anything but be a nice guy. No, she could never forget about everything that had happened but maybe they could finally start fresh.

She closed her eyes and took a deep breath. This was the first day of her new life and she didn't want to waste a moment.

"Happy Birthday to You! Happy Birthday to You!"

Lucia turned to find the entire group standing around Noah in a loose semi-circle while he held a cake blazing with candles. JJ appeared at her side looking harried but gorgeous as always in skinny jeans and stilettos that looked sharp enough to cut glass.

"Sorry I'm late! Noah just told me we were celebrating this morning."

Lucia hugged her close. "It's no problem. Help me blow out the candles?"

After everyone finished the song, they leaned over together and blew out all the candles amid the cheers and shouts of the group. Noah kissed her on the forehead.

"Did you make your wish?" The husky, intimate tone of his voice made her wish she'd taken him up on his offer of staying in bed this morning.

"I don't need wishes. I already have everything I want," she murmured back.

"God, you two need to get a room," JJ interrupted but she was smiling when she said it. It still made Lucia blush though.

"Sorry about her, Boss," Jonas said, coming to stand next to Noah. "I would have left her in the hallway but I didn't want the neighbors to complain about the barking."

JJ swiped at him, but he moved so her fist just barely glanced off his back. He retreated to the kitchen and JJ crossed her arms, probably trying to restrain the urge to chase him down and punch him again. Noah tried to stifle his laughter but the twinkle in his eye gave him away.

"Behave," Lucia whispered before turning to JJ. "Thanks for coming. If I'm getting a do-over, I can't do it without my best friend."

JJ poked out her tongue. "That's what I told Captain America over there when he tried to make me wait until you guys were done singing 'Happy Birthday.'"

Jonas scowled at JJ, even though Lucia had no idea how he'd heard their conversation from where he was standing. Unless he could read lips. Although he would have to be watching them pretty closely for that. She looked between the two of them as the idea took root.

"Jonas seems to annoy you a lot lately, huh?"

"Not really. He just thinks he knows everything. All those steroids are impacting his brain."

Lucia decided to save her suspicions for later. Although the sparks coming from the two weren't easy to ignore, she knew better than anyone that when a man annoyed and excited you like that, it was something you had to figure out on your own.

While Noah cut pieces of cake for everyone, Rafe approached.

"Um, I'll just go see if Noah needs any help." JJ beat a hasty retreat. Lucia wouldn't have been surprised to see skid marks where she'd been standing.

"You make my friends nervous."

"I make everyone nervous. Occupational hazard," Rafe replied easily.

He seemed so at ease with what his life had become but Lucia couldn't help wondering how he'd come to terms with it. Had he ever wanted something different? Perhaps he'd once had dreams of being a chef or an artist. Or maybe opening a flower shop. The idea of her ultra masculine brother surrounded by delicate blooms made her smile.

Rafe tipped his head. "What?"

"Just wondering if you ever wished your life could have been different. Everyone seems so focused on making sure that I'm safe and happy, but what about you? I want you to be happy, too."

He turned and looked at the crowd of people in the kitchen. Oskar and Jonas were stuffing their faces with cake. Matthias stood in the background observing them all like he expected the cake to blow up at any moment. Noah and JJ were deep in conversation about something. Lucia wasn't sure what Rafe saw when looking at them but she saw safety, happiness and love. Did he have those things in his life?

"From the moment our parents died, our life was set to go down a certain path. Poor, young and with limited resources, there weren't too many ways my life could have gone. I knew that eventually I would have to turn to a life of crime to earn enough money to keep you and Nonna safe in our neighborhood. I never expected to have anything more than that."

His answer made her sad. "You deserve to be happy,

Rafe."

"I am. My time in ORUS was fucked up, but I'll never regret the way it happened. They gave me skills I couldn't have learned anywhere else. They gave me the skills to protect the only people that mattered to me."

"I wish I could take care of you, too."

He drew in a breath and Lucia was surprised to see something that looked like tenderness in his eyes. "You do take care of me, Lu. If it wasn't for you, I would have gone down an entirely different path. And I think you do the same for Noah."

"You're really okay about … you know, about us being together?" No matter how old she got, Lucia would never be blasé talking about sex to her big brother.

Rafe pulled her close. "He's been in love with you almost since the moment I brought him home."

Lucia pulled back in surprise. "What? He didn't even know I was alive back then. I had such a crush on him. I would have known if he felt the same way."

Rafe chuckled. "He didn't want you to know. Men like us are afraid to believe in good things. He loved you then, and he loves you now. Plus, I know he'll take care of you. Promise me something."

"Anything."

Unashamed

"Take care of him, too."

She grinned up at him. "I can do that."

Chapter Fourteen

That evening was spent in a haze of singing,
delicious home cooked food and the warmth of being in her

childhood home. Nonna had outdone herself, making one of Lucia's favorites, gnocchi that could melt in your mouth with a special pesto made from a secret family recipe that Nonna guarded fiercely. Lucia figured she wouldn't know exactly what was in it until Nonna whispered it to her from her deathbed.

Hopefully that wouldn't be for another fifty years or so.

"Thank you for dinner, Nonna. And the cake." She hugged her and bent slightly so Nonna could kiss her forehead.

"Take care of yourself, *bambina*. You're all I have left. Well, you and Noah, of course." She included Noah in the statement with a soft smile.

Guilt made Lucia's stomach churn. Once she'd processed the knowledge that her brother was really alive, she'd been thrilled at the idea of telling her grandmother their prayers had been heard. But Rafe had quickly nixed that plan. According to him, it still wasn't safe for Nonna to know he was alive. He'd only come out of hiding because he'd believed Lucia to be in danger.

"I love you, Nonna. So much."

Her grandmother's eyes lit up at the fierce

declaration and she hugged her again before going inside and bolting the door as Noah always insisted she do.

Lucia clutched the cake plate in her hands as they walked back to the car. It was a bitter pill to swallow that the only reason she had Rafe back in her life was because of whoever was trying to hurt her. But she had to have faith that Noah and Rafe could figure this whole thing out. Then Rafe could come out of hiding for real and Nonna would have her grandson back. It was almost too much to wish for but Lucia figured why not? After all, the universe had answered her prayers once before.

As if he could sense her turbulent thoughts, Noah glanced over at her from the driver's seat. "How does it feel to officially be 21?"

"Pretty much the same, except when you drive me nuts, I can officially have a glass of wine. And now, you're less of a dirty old man, so that's a bonus."

Noah's brows snapped down. "I'm not old."

Lucia couldn't help but laugh. "I mean, gosh, you're a whole five years older than me. Ancient. I think I'll upgrade you for some twenty-one-year-old drunken fraternity guy."

Noah laughed as he leaned over the center divide to give her a kiss. His tongue slid past her lips and into her mouth and immediately she was melting. Right into a puddle of hormones. Yeah, he had her number. When he pulled back, his lips tipped up into a smile. "Yeah, good luck with that. You won't find anyone as sexy as me."

She giggled. She carefully maneuvered the pound cake on her lap. "Careful. If you make me spill this cake, we'll both be a sticky mess."

His bark of laughter was sharp. And then she realized what she said. Noah gave her his characteristic wolfish, shameless grin. "I have all kinds of fun ways for us to become sticky messes."

She shook her head. "Noah Blake. You are incorrigible."

"Funny. I've heard that before."

She reached by her feet for the custard sauce that went with the cake and frowned. Where the hell did she put that? Crap. It was still in Nonna's house on the counter. "Noah, I need to go back in the house for the sauce."

Noah shook his head. "Stay here in the car. Lock the doors. I'll get it."

She shook her head and handed him the cake. "Don't be silly. We are literally ten feet from the front door. You're parked right in front of the house. You have perfect sight lines. I'm just going to run in and out. I'll be two seconds. Besides, I know you. You'll run in there, take a bite of something, and get distracted on your way out."

"I will not. And it's not safe."

"Noah, can you see who's coming down the street?"

His lips firmed. "Yes."

"Okay. Remember what we talked about. You will not be unreasonable. Right?"

The muscle in his jaw ticked, but she knew that she'd won. She shoved open the door. "I'll be right back."

To prove to him that she wasn't messing around, she sprinted to the front door, used her key and opened it. Jogging past the living room, she called to her grandmother. "Nonna, I forgot the sauce." But her grandmother was nowhere in the living room, the dining room, or the tiny kitchen. "Nonna?"

It was then that Lucia saw the back door open. Had her grandmother run out with the garbage? No. Noah had taken the garbage out already, before they left.

Lucia's instinct said run. Every part of her said run out front and call for Noah. Then she saw the smudge of blood on the doorframe, and another instinct took over. The one that wanted to protect. Protect the woman who'd given her whole life to raise her. Lucia grabbed a knife out of the knife holder and ran out the back door.

She was met with pitch black. The back porch light was out. Or, someone had put it out. "Nonna? Are you back here?"

She wasn't sure why she was scared. There was no way into the backyard from any location. The back wall was far too high, and Noah had made sure there was glass and barbed wire over the top of it so no one would dare to climb over. The damn thing was twelve feet tall.

And then she saw it, as the moonlight glinted on a shard of glass. Blood. Oh God. Someone had climbed over. The blood on the doorjamb, it hadn't been Nonna's. Lucia whipped around to run back into the house, mouth open ready to scream. And then someone clamped a hand over her mouth.

"For someone I didn't train myself, you are incredibly difficult to kill." The voice was low, icy. It sent a shudder through her body.

Lucia wiggled and struggled in his arms, but he was too strong, overpowering her movements easily.

"All you have to do is die. One hit out on one little girl. But nearly a month later, that little girl is still alive. I have half a mind to ask you how you've done it. Of course, you have Leo watching out for you. And Perseus. But I know for a fact that they're rusty. After I sent Aries after you, you should be dead. It's okay. Sometimes you have to take care of things yourself."

Oh God. This was the guy. This was the guy who was trying to kill her. He slowly released his grip on her mouth. But only by a little. The moment he gave her enough wiggle room, she opened her mouth and bit.

He released her instantly. "Motherfucker."

Lucia didn't wait. With the knife she'd taken from the kitchen firmly in her grip, she rotated her wrist and stabbed it backward. She didn't know what she'd hit. All she knew was she hit flesh. And then she was running.

"Noah! Noah! He's trying to —"

Even as her feet hit the back wooden steps, making a *clop clop clop* noise, Noah was charging through the kitchen at a dead run. Instinctively, she turned to her side, making herself as flat against the railing as possible. At his current velocity, he'd run right into her, and she would not survive that kind of hit.

She turned her head to look behind her. The man with the raspy voice was already attempting to make it around the front of the house.

"I got him in the leg. And bit him. He's bleeding.

Unashamed

Did you see Nonna?"

As he ran, all she heard was Noah saying, "Nonna's safe. He had her tied in the closet."

Noah didn't even bother with the stairs, just made the leap gracefully, smoothly, and was rounding the corner of the house in seconds. Where she stood, Lucia shook, leaning against the railing. How could she have been so stupid? She should've listened to Noah and let him come in with her.

She ran back to the house and found her grandmother on the couch. Duct tape still hung from the side of her face and she rubbed her wrists.

"Nonna."

Her grandmother's eyes went wide as she sagged with relief. "Lucia, you're safe. Thank God. That horrible man. I hope Noah rips his balls off."

Lucia's mouth hung open at her grandmother's use of the word balls.

Nonna's eyes tracked over to Noah who came back through the back door. "Lucia, I need you to get some of Nonna's things. She's coming with us."

Lucia nodded. "Noah, I'm sorry. I should've—"

"Don't. Do not apologize. You did well out there.

And I know the rules. I should've come in with you. Or come myself. Something."

"I thought it would be safe. That no one could get into the back. I can't believe he scaled the back wall."

Noah frowned but stepped right up to her and pulled her close. "That was Orion. He's the man who trained me. And he will do absolutely anything that he has to do to get the job done."

Lucia shook in his arms. "Oh God. What are we going to do?"

Noah's voice was calm. "I'm going to kill him. Before he ever comes near you again."

His tone was so final, so sure. And she knew he meant it.

Lucia was exhausted.

For the time being, they'd put Nonna in Matthias's room and Matthias on the couch. Noah had a place in upstate New York, in a little town called Hope. In the morning, he'd be sending her grandmother there with a friend of his to make sure she was safe. At least for the time being.

They'd both agreed not to tell her that Rafe was alive just yet. They needed to work all of it out first. Although, it killed Lucia not to say anything.

Noah kissed her shoulder. "I know it's hard not to tell her. But that has to be his decision. And in the way that he wants to do it."

"I know. But she deserves to know. That's her grandson. She thinks he's dead. I feel like I'm lying."

Noah shook his head. "Let's deal with one crisis at a time. Right now, you're safe. Nonna is safe. And shocker of shockers, so is Rafe."

"Speaking of my brother, has he called?"

Noah shook his head and pulled her to lie down in the bed next to him. "No. But I left a message about what happened. Told him to be on red alert."

This was hard. Too hard.

Noah's phone chimed with a series of beeps. "Speak of the devil."

Lucia set up. "What is that?"

Noah held up a finger and waited for another series of chimes. "It's Rafe."

A moment later, his phone rang, and Noah answered and put the phone on speaker.

"I see old habits die hard."

"I figured since we've had some trouble, it would be safer."

"That's the understatement of the century. We had some trouble tonight. Orion tried to grab Lucia."

"Motherfucker."

Lucia spoke up. "Rafe, I'm safe. Okay?"

There was a moment of silence. And then her brother spoke. "Where did he try and grab her?"

Noah pursed his lips but he still told the truth. "From Nonna's. He tried to take her right out of the backyard. Lucia managed to stab him, so he's hurt."

There was another string of inventive curses from her brother. And then when he spoke, his voice was low, deadly. "I will kill him."

"I'll fight you for the honor," Noah said. "But first we need to find him. I feel like I've only got half the picture here. I know who would've called in a hit on her, but that doesn't explain why Orion would take the job. That's never happened. At least not as long as I was in ORUS."

"Well, I might have the answer for that," Rafe said.

"You know that shell corporation that Perseus is looking for?"

Lucia frowned. "Perseus?"

Noah shook his head. "Perseus is Matthias's codename."

Lucia could only blink. "Okay, carry on."

"The kid has been digging deeper on that Del Tino property. Turns out when we looked even closer at that shell corporation, HoloCorp, there was another owner. One with ties to cartels all over the world. I started digging through my old FBI case files and some things don't add up. Up until now, every hit we'd taken was essentially because Orion gave it to us. This hit in particular doesn't make sense. Why would they take this kind of drastic action? They're in the wind. Someone poking around is a loose end, but the family doesn't have anything to lose at this point. They wouldn't care if someone found out they owned that house at some point. But there is someone who would."

Noah frowned. "Who?"

"Think about it. The one person who has everything to lose. The one person who exposed himself tonight."

Lucia wasn't getting it, but clearly Noah was

because he stood.

"Fuck. Fuck, fuck, fuck."

Rafe laughed on the other line. "I see you've expanded your vocabulary. Very nice."

Noah ran his hands through his hair. "Orion. All this time. It's been him."

"Right now, that's where my research is pointing. I've gone back through all my old case files to right around the time that I joined. The time the Feds put me undercover, a few of those hits directly threatened ORUS. Yes, those targets were dangerous. Yes, lots of people would have been hurt, but their demise opened up specific strategic holes that ORUS could fill."

Lucia didn't get any of this. "So what does this mean?"

Noah turned to her, his mouth grim. "This means we need to kill Orion."

Her brother agreed. "Yes, preferably, take the fight to him."

Lucia understood now. "So I don't suppose either one of you knows exactly where to find him?"

Noah shook his head. "That is the real problem. Nobody knows that information."

Unashamed

Rafe was more optimistic. "But I think I can get it."

Lucia looked from the phone to Noah and back again. Yes, somebody was trying to kill her, but she knew with her brother and Noah by her side she would survive this.

Chapter Fifteen

Unashamed

A gentle breeze sent the hair that Noah had neglected to get trimmed brushing over his forehead. The sky outside their rented hut on the beach was dotted with fluffy white clouds and reflected the color of the turquoise water. When he'd decided to take his lady on vacation, all he'd wanted was a chance to get her away from the stress and bad memories of the city. He couldn't have gotten a better escape.

Although it wasn't usually considered ideal to bring a group of your best friends along on a romantic getaway.

"I'm going to take a shower now that Matthias is done. Then we can go out to eat. I've been dreaming about that fried fish we had on the beach last night."

Lucia stood from her chair next to his where they'd been relaxing and taking in the view while the rest of the team took turns cleaning up. The guys had a hut next door but they still spent most of their time hanging around Lucia. Now that they'd gotten used to protecting her, Noah suspected they found it just as difficult to turn off their overprotective tendencies where she was concerned. He couldn't blame them for not being able to stay away.

He found her pretty irresistible as well.

"Want me to wash your back?" He wiggled his eyebrows when he said it mainly because it always made her laugh. The joke was on him because her pupils dilated slightly and the look she gave him could only be described as … hungry.

"Later, once we're alone. Then I'll let you wash anything you want."

She left behind the scent of coconut oil and strawberries, which brought a smile to Noah's face. Briefly, he considered the idea of not going back. Sure, she'd miss friends and family back in the city, but perhaps he could convince her it was worth it. They could travel the globe, beach-hopping, and then they'd always be one step ahead of ORUS.

"You look pretty relaxed for a guy with a target on his back," Matthias commented as he took the seat Lucia had vacated.

Noah shook his head. He was truly out of it if he hadn't heard Matthias approach.

"Not relaxed so much as resigned. Men like me don't get a happily ever after. I've always known that. But I'd hoped I could do better than that for Lucia."

Matthias glanced behind them. "You know I've been trying to crack ORUS's internal security codes ever since we got out. It's some of the most sophisticated encryption in existence and almost impossible to crack unless you have someone on the inside."

"Is that right? Too bad we don't know anyone like that."

Matthias grunted. "That's what I thought, too. Until last week."

"What happened last week?" Noah kept his voice steady and calm as if they were discussing something mundane like the weather. Any of the other tourists walking the beach would see nothing more exciting than two guys shooting the breeze and watching the ocean.

"A little bird dropped a piece of information in my lap last week that changed everything." Matthias rested his right foot casually on his left knee. "What would you do if you could find Orion?"

The air around them seemed to solidify and Noah had to concentrate to get his next breath in. Matthias was a straight shooter and not the type to engage in what-if games just for shits and giggles.

"Find him as in know his government identity?"

"Not just his government identity but his fucking street address where he lays his head every night. Where he puts out his trash every Thursday and plants pansies every spring."

Noah looked him straight in the eye. "I would kill him. Immediately and without hesitation."

Matthias nodded and for a few minutes they continued watching the water without conversation. Just when Noah thought he'd scream in frustration, Matthias leaned over and handed him a folded slip of paper.

"Don't say I never gave you anything."

Matthias stepped onto the sand and walked toward the ocean, the breeze lifting his dark hair. When he reached the water's edge, he dipped his bare feet in. Then he looked over his shoulder at Noah and waved.

Noah waved back.

It was all so simple.

A quiet suburban neighborhood. Upscale. If there were cars parked on the street, they were BMWs and Mercedes. A Range Rover here, an Audi there. It was the kind of place that a tech developer might live, or a stockbroker. Refined, elegant. It was not the kind of place people assumed an assassin would live.

Unashamed

Noah used Matthias's fancy tech toys to turn on the jammer. There'd be no calls out of Orion's house tonight. He waited until he saw Orion's blond girlfriend climb into her car and drive down the street. He wanted to make sure she was gone and wouldn't be coming back for anything she might've left at the house.

At first, he'd been shocked to see the blonde walking around in the house through the windows. She'd been waiting on him. Taking care of him. Or maybe she wasn't his girlfriend at all. Maybe she was from a home health service, one where you could hire some hot girl to come and look after you. Generally, he'd call that an escort service, but he didn't judge.

Next order of business was to turn off the security system. That was more difficult, and required Matthias's help.

"Kid, you there?"

"I'm reading you loud and clear, Noah. Are you ready?"

"Yep, I'm here."

"Hold up the red remote to his lock and let me take care of the rest."

Since Orion had one of those smart houses, hacking

would be slightly easier. Although, since he would've added his own layer of security, Noah was ready for all kinds of special booby-traps. He wasn't really interested in Orion knowing he was coming for him.

"Okay, you should be all good."

Riding the razor's edge of anticipation and adrenaline, Noah tried the door. And sure enough, there was no alarm. And no sound, which suited him just fine.

He found Orion in the kitchen. The guy was cooking. As if he hadn't just tried to take out Noah's girlfriend. The woman he loved. His reason for breathing.

"You know, I'm surprised to find that you cook. I assumed you would get one of those shitty meal delivery services."

Orion seemed completely unperturbed. Considering an ex-operative was standing in his home. With a gun at the ready.

"Noah, I wondered when I'd see you again. I am a little surprised to find you in my home, unannounced, but it's not like me to be a rude host. Would you like a drink?"

"No, I think I'll pass. What I want is the code generator and the sat phone."

Orion laughed. "What do you want those for? Only the director of ORUS has those. You know the rules. And there is no way you're making it past biometric scans to steal it."

Noah just gave him a slight smile. "So how long?"

Orion didn't play coy. "Since I became Orion. I've always had my own little side projects. I started to see the real advantage of taking out certain players years ago. Before Libra had to go and get involved. But then, he lost his life for that."

"I actually believed in what ORUS stood for. You had us all believing."

"That's because I'm a leader. You think you can run ORUS? You haven't got what it takes. You've gone soft. The fact that I could even get to Lucia tells me you don't deserve this."

Orion might think that Noah was rusty, but his reflexes were razor-sharp. When Orion sent the knife toward his chest, Noah sidestepped easily. He fired one shot from his gun, the silencer dampening the sound, and hit his target in the shoulder.

"Fuck you. Clearly you don't even know how to make the kill shot anymore."

Orion sent another knife. This one came slightly closer, but that was how Noah wanted it. He fired another shot, this time grazing Orion's ear. He frowned and touched the bloody spot at his ear.

"Oh, so now you're showing off. I'm still not going to give you what you want."

"Yes. You will."

"Oh really? Why would I do that? You'll never have it."

Noah fought with the part of him that wanted to take his time. That wanted to incapacitate Orion enough that he could tie him to a chair and play. But he suppressed the part of him that liked to kill. He wasn't letting that part of himself out anymore. Not ever.

This was a job. Clean, simple. He had one goal. And it wasn't retribution. It was a matter of safety. He took aim and hit Orion's other shoulder. And his former boss cursed again.

"You might not want to give me the code, but I'm taking it one way or the other."

A series of throwing stars came his way, but he saw that they caused Orion significant pain to wield them. One of them clipped Noah in the shoulder. He barely felt the burn. And bonus, Orion had to step out from around the island to fire them off. And then Noah saw his opening. With one perfectly placed shot, he hit Orion in the exact place Lucia had stabbed him. His former boss went down in a heap.

Without preamble, Noah walked over calmly and dragged Orion up by the arm.

Orion writhed and tried to get away, but Noah was having none of it. Thanks to the schematics Matthias had found, locating the safe was easy enough. When Orion tried to fight him, Noah calmly but efficiently sent a blow to the back of his skull, forcing him to collapse. The biometric scan was easy. One handprint. Done.

The eye scan was a little trickier as he had to hold Orion up, awkwardly bracing him against the wall with the panel. Noah leaned his head back and pried an eyelid open. And when he had the clear scan, he let Orion fall to the ground as the safe clicked open.

Noah turned the latch, and inside there were several papers and exactly what he was looking for. He took the sat phone and the code generator, as well as the stack of papers in there. Then he turned back to Orion and fired one kill shot to the head.

He had more work to do tonight.

When Ian came out of the shower, he stopped mid-stride when he saw Noah standing in the middle of his room. Anyone else would have shit a brick to see an uninvited guest in their locked home in the middle of the night, but Ian just shrugged and then walked to his dresser where he calmly selected a shirt and jeans.

"So I guess my number finally came up, huh? Just make it fast, kid. I think you owe me that much."

Noah chuckled. Ian had always been such a grumpy bastard, but no one could call him anything less than a professional. He wasn't the type to whine and beg for his life. Truth be told, the idea of dying at the hands of a friend was probably Ian's idea of an honorable death.

"I'm not here to take you out. Who would I call when I need advice?"

Ian pushed up his sleeves and leaned against the dresser. "What's the occasion? Don't tell me you missed my pretty face?" He stroked the edge of his scarred jaw absently.

"I was in the neighborhood."

"This place was locked up tighter than the Pentagon. Or so I thought anyway. My guys are good, too."

"Matthias is better."

Ian didn't bother arguing. They both knew it was the truth. Noah looked around the room, taking in the minimalist décor and looking toward the closet with the military grade weapons that he'd checked out while Ian was in the bathroom. Once he made this decision, there was no undoing it. But Ian had worked alongside him many times and taught him a lot along the way. He was a sonofabitch, no doubt about it, but he was fair and once upon a time had actually believed in the original mission of ORUS.

After a short pause, he pulled up his sleeve to reveal the series of connected dots that formed his ORUS identification. Ian's eyes fell to his own exposed wrists.

"Phoenix," Noah said. "Your name is strangely prophetic."

"What does that mean?"

His mind made up, Noah pulled the sat phone and code generator from the interior pocket of his jacket and set them carefully on the desk. Such innocuous items to hold such power.

Ian stood up straight. The items didn't exactly

broadcast what they were, but Noah figured the other man knew something was up just by how strangely he'd been behaving.

"It's time to change your tattoos. You're Orion now."

"What the hell?"

For the first time, Noah had the supreme pleasure of seeing Ian smile. Just as quickly, his face returned to its usual sullen expression.

"I hope you know what you're doing, kid."

The name brought a smile to Noah's face, reminding him of how he talked to Matthias. It had been so long since he'd felt like a kid, where everything was fresh and new. When everything was possible.

But now it was. And he wasn't going to waste a single moment.

"What I'm doing is something that should have been done long ago. The original goal and purpose of ORUS has been twisted for profit long enough. Now things are going to be different. It's time for control to be back with the people who believed that we could do some good."

Ian held out a hand and when they shook, Noah could feel it. They were starting something solid. Something right.

"Good luck, kid." Ian paused and then asked, "Do you really think it's possible for men like us to get a second chance? The ORUS I was trained to serve is a shadow organization at its core. You really think we can turn this around?"

"First, I'm not turning it around. You are. And I believe you can do it."

Ian's eyes rounded. "You're really out? For good?"

An image of Lucia waiting for him in their bed, all bright eyes and smooth skin, spread warmth and contentment through him until he felt like he could have actually walked on air.

"Some men can exist in that place between the dark and the light. But I'm tired of being in the shadows. From now on I'm walking in the light."

With one last handshake, Noah walked out and into a future where anything seemed possible.

THANK YOU for reading *Unashamed*, the final

book of the exciting new romantic misadventure trilogy, *Shameless*.

We told you Noah Blake was #SHAMELESS. We hope you enjoyed Noah and Lucia's story. Find out now how the Blake Security Saga continues with JJ & Jonas's story, #FORCE. Preorder Now at malonesquared.com

Shameless

ABOUT THE AUTHORS

New York Times & USA TODAY Bestselling author **M. MALONE** lives in the Washington, D.C. metro area with her three favorite guys: her husband and their two sons. She holds a Master's degree in Business from a prestigious college that would no doubt be scandalized at how she's using her expensive education. j

Independently published, she has sold more than 1/2 million ebooks in her two series THE ALEXANDERS and BLUE-COLLAR BILLIONAIRES. Since starting her indie journey in 2011 with the runaway bestselling novella "Teasing Trent", her work has appeared on the New York Times and USA Today bestseller lists more than a dozen times.

She's now a full-time writer and spends 99.8% of her time in her pajamas.

minxmalone.com

USA Today Bestselling Author, **NANA MALONE**'s love of all things romance and adventure started with a tattered romantic suspense she borrowed from her cousin on a sultry summer afternoon in Ghana at a precocious thirteen. She's been in love with kick butt heroines ever since.

With her overactive imagination, and channeling her inner Buffy, it was only a matter a time before she started creating her own characters. Waiting for her chance at a job as a ninja assassin, Nana, meantime works out her drama, passion and sass with fictional characters every bit as sassy and kick butt as she thinks she is.

nanamaloneromance.net

88442889R00140

Made in the USA
Columbia, SC
30 January 2018